Travel Is So Broadening

Travel Is So Broadening

Wasela Hiyate

QUATTRO BOOKS

The publication of *Travel Is So Broadening* has been generously supported by the Canada Council for the Arts and the Ontario Arts Council.

Author photo: Jason Ainsworth
Editor: Anne Cunningham
Cover design and typography: Natasha Shaikh

Library and Archives Canada Cataloguing in Publication

Hiyate, Wasela, author
        Travel is so broadening / Wasela Hiyate.

Short stories.
ISBN 978-1-927443-82-8 (paperback)

        I. Title.

PS8615.I93T73 2015   C813'.6   C2015-906040-0

Published by Quattro Books Inc.
Toronto
www.quattrobooks.ca

Printed in Canada

Bizarre travel plans are dancing lessons from God.
  – Kurt Vonnegut

You go away for a long time and return a different person –
you never come all the way back.
  – Paul Theroux

The open road is the school of doubt in which man learns faith
in man.
  – Pico Iyer

Walking is a virtue, tourism is a deadly sin.
  – Bruce Chatwin

Because in the end, you won't remember the time you spent
working in the office or mowing your lawn. Climb that
goddamn mountain.
  – Jack Kerouac

Contents

In Memoriam

Gregory Thomas Love (October 9, 1973 - April 20, 2008)

Goyo, que èste libro sea nuestro niño.

THE MONKEYS IN SONGKHLA

It looks like that piece of luggage with all my clothes in it is really gone. The airline's no help 'cause the stewardesses all talk to me in half-Thai, then to Don when he starts nodding; his broken Thai fixing their broken English. How would they know I'm Korean, or a Kap? At least that's what my Dad thinks of me. As if it wasn't partly his fault – the jeep he leased for me, the tennis lessons he tried to keep up when I went away to school. Dad's all like, *Ayah! We're in Canada now. You go to school and work hard. Mix with the right people.* He had to give up the jeep, but I still have memories of those nights with the girls – whistling at guys with the top pulled down, pumping tunes, the wind flipping our hair wild. Yeah, I did some studying too. Now I've got this big-ass student loan I'm trying to pay off.

Most of the kids in the guest house are from Canada, the States, the U.K. – digging the hippie lifestyle, living in this country on next to nothing. I bet some of them even get their pogey sent here. You see them all on Khao San drinking beer in those bars with Hollywood movies blaring all night – the boys with their little goatees and the girls in sundresses and ponytails. I'm still so freaked out by the heat and the smell of the Chao Phraya that winds through the city, and the language – everything – it's such a sudden change that I barely pay attention to any of the people we meet on the first night we're out for dinner. Don and I are drinking with a bunch from the hostel, and when we walk out all together on the street, we see the Thais ignoring the *farang*, but when Don and I walk by hand in hand, they stare.

"They think you're pretty Western-looking for a ho," Don says.

Can't they see my wedding ring? Then they'll think Don saved me. Funny, 'cause the way I remember it, I saved him. From himself – his own apathy. But that's when I start seeing it – all the emaciated junkies or pot-bellied tourists holding hands with Thai girls, buying them food and beer and ice cream.

We're not here on vacation, really – we're going to teach English, we explain to the group at the next restaurant. I'm finally able to feel my appetite and greedily scarf down the noodles on my plate. The next day Don and I target a couple of the big English academies. We figure with my degree, teaching certificates and experience, I'll do well and so will Don, although he never finished his B.A. The staff at the guest house treat him with a lot of respect for a skinny Canadian kid. The guys all want to be friends with him, tell him jokes in Thai since he still remembers some of the phrases he learned from when he lived with his host family all those years ago in some cultural exchange program. That's Don: big whitey who's always into what else is out there. The girls are flirty when they talk to him, then I get their curiosity, sometimes their respect by default – for just being with him, or the irked surprise that says *What the? She's not so pretty...*

One of the schools has us fill in one of their applications, which asks Father's Occupation. *Write doctor or lawyer... just do it!* Don whispers. So I print doctor. He takes the lawyer angle. Then we hand in our resumes and the number at the guest house. We have a tourist day in Bangkok since I need to get some clothes – who knows when the airline will find my bag. We stroll past the gold shops where all the deformed beggars line the street, make you feel like shit for even thinking of buying a gold chain. Don buys some roasted grasshoppers. *What? They're a delicacy here*, he says when I pull a face at his offer. I buy all of these girly clothes. The vendors get a kick out of having me try on the workpants and wraps and some of those matching blue or pink or yellow suits all the office girls wear with their white pumps. I see them in the early morning going to work, sitting in back of their motorcycle taxis. Wow, Thai women are beautiful. It's a demure beauty that matches the sweetness of their voices, *kaa*. Yes. Then the way the men in the shops smoke cigarettes and drink Johnny Walker all afternoon, *krap!* Yes! A macho shout. Almost militant.

We head to the noodle stands in the evening, though my stomach is fucking with me again – it's pretty common here with the intense heat and me not knowing how much water to drink, or to stay out of the sun. Still, having to run to the bathroom twice in one meal is silly. Don says according to the travel book we should have gotten shots. We didn't come prepared, just rushed out of those Montreal January winds. It took us forever to save enough. We figure the real money will come when we're in Japan, but the beaches of Thailand were so much more welcoming, we came here first. Just booked our flights, and *hello* golf course airstrip. Or should I say, *sawasdi*.

"Stay out with me. The air will do you some good," Don says while he's walking me back to the guest house.

"You go, I'm still tired from all that shopping."

"Just come – if you don't, I'll get hit on all night. Everyone has a picture in their pockets of some girl who can *suck good dick*."

"Yeah, that must bite," I caress his groin playfully. He starts laughing, turns around and checks to make sure no one's looking, pins me to the wall of a shop for some x-rated necking, then we're both hurrying back to the guest house and our room. We don't leave the guest house again until late that night. And all I know is it's sure true what they say about vacation sex.

The next day we decide to check out Wat Pho. A group of girls passes us on the streets with Leonardo DiCaprio's pretty face on their t-shirts. We enter the monastery and peek into the temple with the golden Buddha reclining inside. There are marigolds everywhere. Outside, they've already started the shadow-puppet play. We stake out a piece of ground, spread a blanket and lounge. People look at us. Maybe we're sitting too close together? I play with my ring self-consciously. Maybe I play with it so they'll know – *this isn't just for the week, I'm his for life.*

My eyes open in the dark, humid air of our room. Over the rhythmic whirr of the ceiling fan, Kieto, the brush-haired concierge, shouts, "Don, telephone!" There is a quick series of knocks.

Don opens the door and Kieto spies me, naked under the sheets, then lurches away from the view as if he'll burst into flames for just looking at Don's wife. "Okay. In a minute, *kap koon krap.*" Don thanks him, hurries into a pair of pants and rushes out of the room. He's back in five minutes, all excitement. "Guess who's got an interview tomorrow at the Academy!"

"For both of us?"

"I asked about you and they said they couldn't accept your application."

"Why not?"

"I don't know. Maybe they only need one teacher."

We walk through the hot morning after breakfast, the egg, rice, *nam plaa* – fish water, and instant coffee still in my mouth. We pass a group of people on the steps of the school – teachers. They're all dressed in white shirts and beige pants, though the one woman among them wears a dress. When the Academy director, a Thai woman dressed in a smart skirt suit calls Donald Vickers, her eyes flit across me, and there's something like a smirk that almost lands on her lips. She takes him into a glass office and they seem to have a friendly conversation. I watch her toss her red-tinged hair – the same as mine – she crosses and uncrosses her legs so that the long slit of her black skirt opens each time. I stand up, yawn, stretch, notice that Don has become very excited, waving his arms around. The two of them are discussing something seriously now, since an expression of fake sympathy replaces the come-on smile she had before. Then she rises to shake his hand.

Don's got tight lips when he walks over to join me. "They won't hire you because you're not white."

"What?"

"I know. I tried talking to her. She says the students won't take you seriously. She says we can live here decently on just my wages."

"Yeah, I dunno ..." This takes me completely by surprise. It hadn't occurred to me that besides status, race would be an issue. Not here, of all places.

"Anyway she told me I can let her know on Monday. At first she was trying to convince me to take a post near Patpong – because obviously every guy who comes here is just dying to work in the red light district," he says ironically. "She also said they have a branch in Songkhla. Wouldn't be so bad living near the beach, eh? And you might be able to teach children there."

But all I can think is I'm not ready to be running around after little kids, coming home from work exhausted, making half of what Don makes for a two-hour class with adults.

We go to Chatuchak the next day. Don knows how much I like markets – so much to see and smell, crafts to fondle and snacks to sample. And so many pictures to take of people in their stalls. I love the place. Don goes off to look at antique Buddhas, and I take out the guidebook and read about the Gulf provinces, see the pictures of its turquoise water and white sand beaches. Soon I'm starting to like the idea of staying and letting Don make the bucks.

"What are you going to tell them?" I ask him when he comes back.

"Who?"

"The school. Are you taking the job?"

"I don't know, should I?"

"Well, if you do, you can't ever be pissed off at me for not working, 'cause I don't know if I want to teach kids right now."

"You take care of me and I'll take care of you." He takes my hand in his. We go to the crafts area and buy tapestries and pillow covers to mail home to friends and family. I pick up a postcard with a picture of a pristine white sand beach and turquoise water. *Hello from Paradise*, it says. I scribble something to Tina and my parents and we mail it once we're back in town near the guest house.

Don tells the Academy he'll check in at the Songkhla branch the following week. We take the train south, and I'm happy to be out of the loud bustle of Bangkok, watching the tiny villages flitting past, the forests of rubber and banana trees. I'm dressed in the wrap workpants, wearing my Birkenstocks with them, not flip-flopping around like the villagers. I've only ever been this aware of being an Asian chick while walking around the east part of Montreal a few times. I don't think I look Thai – but there is a Chinese population here too. Who knows what they think? All I know is that I've never been worried about being taken for a prostitute before.

We trundle out of the train station in Songkhla with all of our bags, catch a *tuktuk* to the guest house. The sky's unreal it's so clear, and when we're on the seaside road I can't believe the intensity of the azure water and sky and the smell of the ocean air.

"Holy shit!" I say, because the view really looks like some vacation brochure. Don laughs at me 'cause I keep saying: "Oh my God, it's so beautiful!"

I change into my bikini right away while Don unpacks. It's 2:00 in the afternoon, and the sun is blazing. There's hardly anyone on the sand, only two people walking along the water holding hands in the distance: a man with his daughter. There's a small restaurant that starts a strip of beach establishments to the left. No one's in the patios. I'm already in the water when I see Don run to the beach.

"Be careful running around like that – at least put on a t-shirt!" He lays his towel out and drops a bag on the ground, chugs from the water bottle. I'm bobbing on the water, waving at him. But he's looking at the guy with the daughter as they come walking up the beach. The guy bends down and kisses the girl on her mouth, grabs her bum, and I'm so shocked I just stand there watching. The two of them walk closer quietly swinging hands and when I look at the girl, she eyes me and Don curiously. She looks young, but seems older as she comes nearer. She's wearing a t-shirt with jeans and flip-flops and shows her perfect dimples to the guy, gives him a smile that breaks your heart. Then I notice the guy she's with isn't Thai at all.

"Dude, what's up? Can't get any at home?" Don says to him.

My heart's racing because I want to kill the guy. I run up to meet Don on the beach and we follow the john and his date: "Well, I like them young and oriental!" Don shouts.

"Can't do it anywhere else 'cause I'd be arrested." I add my two cents.

We know the guy hears us because he starts walking faster. The young woman is alarmed when he speeds up and leaves her a few paces behind. She turns and looks at us like we're nutcases. But after we've chased them down the beach a little while, I don't feel any better. I just stop suddenly in my tracks, standing there all pent up and then the rage falls loose and I'm crying. Don pulls me into the ocean and I feel like I'm acting the wrong part in a commercial for paradise, thinking *what the?* The aquamarine and my tears and the sun all blinding me from different angles. Don paddles around me, makes me laugh with his stupid seal routine. "You feel too much," he says.

"She reminds me of Tina." My 14-year-old little sister has similar dimples in her cheeks that I've always been jealous of.

On the first day of Don's new teaching position, I walk around the town with my resume in my whitest shirt and work skirt. Some of the school administrators look at me, their eyes skit up and down quick as a gecko, tell me they're not hiring right now. I go to Hat Yai and one of the places there takes my resume, but I know from the look on the guy's face that I shouldn't cross my fingers.

After class, Don comes home and I'm reading *The Happy Hooker* because it was the most interesting book in the *farang* bookstore in Bangkok. Then I had to fight Don for it, though he ended up winning and finishing first.

"Can you believe she chooses to fuck a dog instead of a black man?" I ask when he's in the door.

"What?" he puts his bag down and starts unbuttoning his shirt. "Yeah, but that was the apartheid era. She could've been sent to jail for doing the guy."

"Wouldn't they put her in jail for doing the dog? I guess the dog's not gonna tell, right?"

"That stuff is all fake anyway." He steps out of his pants. "Let's get dinner – I'm starving. You wouldn't believe my classes today. Everyone does their homework but it's all wrong! Whether they're university students or businessmen."

I get up, stretch lazily. "Let's have crab," I say, wanting to hit the beach since I'm afraid to go there without Don. He comes out of the shower soaking and starts shaking the water off of him, then he's chasing me around with his dick half-hard, getting the whole room wet, wagging it around like a happy dog. "Give it a suck?"

"Uh, no?"

"Hand job?"

"I thought you were hungry?" I say.

"Come on, just a little tug?" he pleads. "I'll give you a bigger allowance …"

It seems weird that he's not laughing when he says this – kinda takes the fun out of it. "Okay, okay." I get down to business, even take off my top when he asks.

At the restaurant the owner greets us and smiles at Don, asks if he wants a beer. Don's looking at the menu and I'm looking at the sea and the few people who are in the restaurant tonight, mostly tourists. I try not to stare at the young blond guy with his Thai girl. Maybe she really is his girlfriend or co-worker or something. The owner's daughter comes to the table with a pad of paper. She's about eleven years old and wears lipstick and nail polish and gives Don long looks that make me laugh. He orders for us, then tells me about class. "I don't think I've ever been taken this seriously before. It's bizarre. But hey, I'm not complaining. Maybe I'll do something fun in class tomorrow, just to loosen everyone up."

"I brought my all-purpose activity package," I say. "You can take a look when we get back."

I get up to use the bathroom – only once during the meal. I guess I'm finally getting used to the food. When I get back, the owner has taken my place at the table and I can hear Don's polite laugh, not his big guffaw. The owner turns my way and stands suddenly, his grin so wide I can count his gold teeth. I take my seat. Don gives me an incredulous look as he watches the owner leave. "The guy ... he asked if we wanted to adopt his daughter, or take her back to the guest house so she could help clean up, help out in any way ..."

"Oh my God."

"Yeah." He raises his brow.

"No wonder she's all dressed up," I say.

We stroll the beach. "I'm in paradise with all the cheap beer and quality young pussy here!" I shout to all the johns who can understand English. Some of them look at me like I'm mentally disturbed and might go running at them at any moment.

The next day I'm walking around the village in my most *farang* clothes. Beige shorts and Birks and white t-shirt. Seriously, all I need is the Tilley hat. I'm walking around the village to the Wat. There are no saffron robes around and as I peek in to look at the idols I wonder what it'd be like living here, shaved head, begging alms like the nuns in the market I've seen in Bangkok. The sun is midday hot and I've forgotten my water bottle, but I sit on the gazebo near the entrance.

Suddenly a macaque drops from a tree, then another, then another. They look at me with their swollen little bellies and pink hairy faces. I stand up because in no time, there's a lot of them. And I don't want to freak out but I can't help it. It's an odd experience, being surrounded by monkeys. There's no glass like at the zoo. They're so used to seeing tourists and being fed by them that they expect a snack from me too, and I have nothing in my purse. The little macaques start scratching, acting all nonchalant, though I know they're waiting.

I stand up, start moving through them very slowly – not wanting to frighten them in case they get all Hitchcock on me or something. Finally I'm on the street again and walking quickly, not daring to look around to see if any of them have decided to follow me. I smile at the villagers and they look at me blankly. Some nod.

While I'm heading back to the guest house it hits me: maybe if I taught kids I could somehow reach them, help them.

The next night Don comes back much later than usual.

"The guys wanted to take me out for a drink. We went to one of those bars in Hat Yai. Jesus. I was wrong about small towns – at least this one."

I'm already in bed with a firm plan in my head to talk to the junior school principal the next day. Don runs the shower and I don't even notice when he crawls into bed 'cause I'm already out.

I wake up when he pushes himself inside me.

"I just need to relax," he says in my ear, and I can smell the alcohol on his breath, feel him burning inside me. I try to throw him off.

He pins my arms; his whole body bears down on me so my legs are buried in the mattress and I feel a panic rushing through my whole body though I can't move. "Please," I choke.

He keeps going.

Finally, I get out of the bed. I can't stop trembling even when I wrap myself in the extra blanket and I'm in the bathroom retching, but I'm only dry heaving – nothing's coming up. I lie on the floor, towels tucked under me, curled around the toilet. I wake up when the dawn light hits the blue tile and go back to bed, lie as far away from Don as I can manage. When he's up getting ready for work and closes the door behind him, I fall asleep.

I get to the school very late in the day. By the time I'm there, the director has already left and I find myself wandering the village alone, in my professional Thai woman outfit. People look at me curiously – recognizing that the day before I was just a tourist. I head back to the guest house and the concierge says there's a message for me. Someone's going to hire me! I'll be working by next week! I ask for details and he explains that the airline has found my bag, that they're holding it for whenever I can pick it up. The disappointment sinks in my gut. I run up to the room and put on my bathing suit. *I'm allowed to show my body. I'm allowed to fucking swim if I want!*

The water is cold and salty and stings my eyes. There are *farang* and Thai men and Thai girls walking up and down the beach all afternoon, but I ignore them, float on the water gazing at the sky, tan myself into a golden Buddha.

Don comes home on time. I'm downstairs, watching TV with the desk boy, seeing all the guests who come and go.

"*Sawasdi krap,*" Don says to us.

I just look at him and turn back to the program.

"Coming up?" he asks.

"Not for a while," I say without taking my eyes from the television.

"Are you hungry?"

"I already ate," I lie.

By the time Don comes down the stairs again, I'm starving. He's dressed in a linen shirt I picked out for him last summer, and his shorts and sandals and sunglasses – so Ralph Lauren. He takes my hand as he walks past, pulling me with him. I yank my hand back, keeping up with his pace. He shoots me a look, shakes his head. "I can't believe I got so wasted last night. I swear, they all wanted to take me out and personally buy me a drink. I could barely remember my name by the time I got home."

"You don't remember anything?"

"I recall lots of naked women doing strange tricks ..."

We're walking along in silence and it seems stupid to push the subject of last night. We get to the beach restaurant with the eleven year-old waitress. She's already serving two tables when we take a seat. Her father chats amiably with an old Australian man drinking a highball, clinking his ice around every now and again before sipping. We order the usual curry crab and tom yam and she brings Don a Singha beer, so I order one too and she's surprised. "Alright, you can have one beer tonight," Don jokes, as if he's keeping count in his head of how much dinner's going to cost.

When our waitress brings the food, I see the man at the bar is eyeing her like she's also a tasty dish. In a few minutes they leave the restaurant together and are heading to the house in the back. "Look at that," I nod.

Don turns around. "What?"

"The girl is working double duty tonight."

Don turns back to the food, shovels a hunk of rice and crab into his mouth, chews quickly though carefully, and takes a long sip of beer to wash everything down.

"So that's okay with you now?"

"Look, I just want to eat. I've had a long day and I'm tired and hungry."

"Well, I guess we'll both be like that in a couple of days. I'm heading to the junior school to see if they'll give me a job."

"I think that's a great idea," Don says curtly. He looks out at the water. "You'll like it ... it's hard being here and not having a place, a role, somewhere."

"I want to teach sex education."

"I don't think you'll be able to teach them much here!" Don guffaws.

"I mean, teach girls how to protect themselves, how to value themselves ..."

Don is silent for a moment, picks at the food on his plate. "Don't think women's studies will go over so well. Besides, sex tourism means money. Everyone knows that." He's still looking out at the horizon. I watch the sun burn into the sky and water.

We walk along the beach and I find a long piece of sun-bleached bamboo, use it as a walking stick since I'm needing a little extra help to keep me balanced. Don takes off his sandals, steps into the water up to his calves. Later, we're heading to the centre of town and I ask if he's seen the Wat yet. He shakes his head, so I lead him there, bouncing my stick on pavement or grass or earth as we walk. At an intersection, we pass the girl who's got the same dimples as my sister. She's holding hands with a youngish guy who towers over her. He's not the usual ugly john, probably even has a girlfriend back home. We walk past silently. My heart's racing and I turn, lean heavily into my walking stick and shout, "Scumbag!"

Don pulls me along.

"What? I can't say anything?" I yell at him.

"It's just embarrassing ..." he hisses, looking around and smiling at anyone he thinks may have seen. "Try to be a little more Buddhist about this. If you're going to work here, you'll have to fit into the community."

I know I'm looking at him now as if he's crazy. He shakes his head.

We enter the temple grounds and see a few tourists trickling through the gates of the monastery; they look around, walk into the Wat, then out again. We wait in the gazebo and the army of macaques descends from the trees. Don laughs at them. "We should've brought food."

Maybe because I'm the one with the handbag, they come closer to me. I hit the stick on the ground to keep them away.

Then one of them gets too close, so I crack the stick near his legs, but he doesn't get it, maybe thinks I want to play with him or something. He rushes the bench where I'm sitting so I hit him wherever I can get him and somewhere I lose my fear, take the stick with both hands. All the monkeys run away and there's screeching and shrieking and I corner the bugger when he pulls back, keep whacking because he thinks he's going to get away but I won't let him. And the stick feels good and strong in my hand, even makes that hollow bamboo *whooof whooof* as it zings through the air, hitting the little bastard.

Then the monkey's screaming, "Stop it! Stop it!" and I'm *thinking holy shit, Thai monkeys can talk*! Then I realize it's Don who's shouting. The macaque stops cowering and scurries away and I see that he can only limp because his leg is twisted all funny and his head's bleeding.

"Jesus!" Don wipes his face, but the surprise stays. He turns, half-running to the gate, looking behind at the temple for monks.

I'm standing there with the piece of bamboo in my hand, drop it when I see the blood on the end of it. At the temple, I pull off my sandals. It's empty except for a small Buddha and an altar of coconuts and flowers and rice with a lit incense stick. I kneel on the floor and fall forward, still feeling crazy like any minute I'll start screaming and won't be able to stop and people will look at me and Don will be shaking his head in disappointment, will have to apologize to everyone for me and lead me away. But my forehead feels good on the cool temple floor so I pray even though I'm not Buddhist and I don't know Sanskrit or Thai or even Korean really well anymore. I don't know how to help the little monkey or all the girls who may never see a better life until they've been released from this one.

It's dark by the time I walk out the monastery gates. Don's nowhere to be seen. At the bus station, I drop my wedding ring into the hands of a beggar with a face so folded, ravaged by some tropical disease, I'm not even sure she has eyes. My work pants have come loose, and I retie the waist, sling my bag around one side of my neck so it's not just dangling loosely from my shoulder where it's easier for pickpockets and purse-snatchers. I'm carrying everything I really need: my wallet, my cell with the North American plan, my passport. The streets are quiet and I can hear the ocean, feel its salty breeze fresh on my face. I can't wait to change into my clothes at the airport.

MO

Mo cannot take Fridays off. As a result he finds himself praying in the eastbound streetcar on his way to work. He assumes the appropriate position – as if holding the Qu'ran in hand – and enters a meditative state of worship, mumbling to himself at the points where he usually sings when in the privacy of his own room. Mo makes time for prayer five times throughout the day, which isn't difficult since he is assistant manager at his uncle's restaurant and his uncle is a somewhat religious man himself. The plan, explained as such by Uncle Iqbal, involves 1) gaining experience with Canadian clientele which will enable him to speak English more fluently, 2) practising the most recent accounting software and techniques, and 3) giving Mo Canadian work experience. "Very, very necessary," insisted Uncle. "It was bad enough when I first came. You might as well have come straight from the tea plantation! But these days don't you dare grow a beard. You remember what happened to Yusuf." Uncle paused, looked thoughtful. "We'll just keep calling you Mo."

Once the few objectives Uncle outlined are achieved, Mo will be able to find a suitable position as an accountant with a good firm and make use of the diplomas he attained in Pakistan. "It will be difficult for you." The older man tried to comfort Mo with an arm on the shoulder. "It is not like home. Everything here is what they call *ass backwards*, you know. The gays have so much power. They are always on television with their supermodels. Reporters hang on their words longer than the bloody Prime Minister's!"

Mo finds the Canadian language difficult. Not as familiar and *proper* as the British English he learned at school. He always heard the word *proper* itself in the accent of his teachers in the past. There are many confusing terms and phrases, and he cannot guess how long his uncle's goal will take. Mo finds the language is even sillier – more silly? – when referring to food. There were a few products that his British teachers mentioned, with names that made him feel like retching when translated literally. Headcheese. Blood pudding. Or was it black sausage? The latter always made him think of a phallus filled with blood. But in Toronto, the supermarket where Uncle usually shopped was more *haram* than a brothel. Mo saw all types of references to the scavenger animal: pork hocks, pork bellies, pig knuckles. They minced it with fat and cartilage and sold it as sausage. Uncle insisted he could never bring himself to eat such a monstrosity, while Aunty laughed in the kitchen behind him. According to Uncle, all the family restaurants also served the delectable – detestable? – hamburgers and cheeseburgers made with ground-up beef. Even the Hindus would have trouble eating out!

Mo does not understand food in this country. That people with money and some degree of education would enjoy eating their own or other people's pets, minced up in the same fashion as pig and sold on street corners as "hot dogs," makes him hang his head in great embarrassment for Canadians. It seems that people take their dogs very seriously, so it does not make sense. And the sheer variety of dogs – wild and domestic – was shocking: poodles, dachshunds, labradors, alsatians, dalmatians, St. Bernards, beagles, cocker spaniels … Once at the subway station, Mo had seen a black woman in boots and a red scarf walking a dog past a man seated on the floor. The man had moved, stirring about the crumpled newspaper and clothing that surrounded him and had started growling suddenly, scaring the woman. Her dog had barked back at the angry man. Then the man had started yelling about the wild dogs – something about trying to keep out the Chinks, Wops, Yids, Niggers, and Spics. They must really be savage beasts for him to have spit the names with such venom. Still, Mo knew about the raccoons, moose, and the awesome white polar bears, black bears, and grizzly bears, but who would have known that there were packs of wild dogs in Canada too? Perhaps so many of them died each winter that the government was compelled to sell their minced bodies as hot dogs.

It was not just the dogs of the culture that perplexed Mo. Some of the restaurants he'd dined in when meeting his English tutor made his heart heavy for the suffering Canadian people. The university chap always ordered a beer and small bony pieces of chicken wings that greased his lips so they shone throughout the tutorial. Shawn was very interested in teaching in Japan where rich and beautiful women supposedly awaited him. The restaurants he chose served dishes in which spices and herbs were replaced by the heaviness of sugar and salt. And the preferred sauce was a thick red liquid in a bottle that was both sweet and tangy, called ketchup. Canadians oozed – used? – the stuff over everything. Mo watched in fascination while Shawn drowned a plate of French fries in ketchup and vinegar. The tutor responded to Mo's incredulous stare, "What? You have curry sauce, we have this."

Even worse than eating in the restaurants was what came afterwards – the toilet. Mo tried to hold it in during tutorials, but once, during the second meeting, he found himself so uncomfortable and bloated he couldn't concentrate on what Shawn's shiny lips were saying. Having to use the public stall was no problem, but using the paper to smear his waste like peanut butter had been so offensive that he'd cut his tutorial short – in the middle of learning the various rules and usages of the present progressive tense. He'd taken the subway directly to Uncle's house where he'd been given a room in the damp basement, and washed in the shower at a scalding temperature until he was satisfied. Mo lay on his bed, listening to his Uncle's sons upstairs as they cheered, jeered and laughed in front of the television set. Mo cried like a child. Nobody had told him it was going to be like *this*. Now he understood why others who'd gone off to the States called home in tears of frustration, telling family how terrible the living was. It was difficult to do anything in this part of the world *properly*, even keep your bottom clean! If only his mother would visit. She would coo kind and reassuring words, and her cooking was so much better than Aunty's. Mo prayed with each *namaz* for a visit from his mother, or, second best, for a wife.

Mo understands that what this new society may lack in cuisine, it certainly makes up for in friendliness. In this country, everyone works together. His uncle's restaurant is a good example of this Canadian "co-operation" since the porter is from Afghanistan, the dishwasher is, unbelievably, a Hindu from Kerala, and the cook is Ahmed, one of Uncle's friends from Karachi.

Mo looks up through the streetcar window instinctively, a block before his stop. He pulls the cord and fights his way to the rear doors. In the restaurant, Mo finds everyone in front of the television in the kitchen, watching the afternoon report. The American president comes on – the white man who speaks the most nonsensical English Mo has ever heard – and there are groans, pieces of misshapen naan and small chicken bones thrown at the screen.

"My dog's testicles contain more intelligence than that fool," Ahmed brandishes a ladle coated in dhal.

The waitresses roll their eyes when they catch a glimpse of the screen while placing their orders. They're all Canadian girls Uncle Iqbal hired based on their height and grace. He thought it made good business sense to hire white food servers in a country where most of the customers would be white. "One of them is even Jewish," Uncle had announced proudly. She had long ringlets that she shook free from her ponytail at the end of each shift. Mo noticed she also had the largest breasts of them all, a constant, though perhaps pleasant, distraction for his uncle.

"Ask the waitresses to wear these – new policy," Uncle said, a week after Mo was introduced as the new assistant manager. He handed Mo an assortment of colourful *salwar kameez* outfits with matching *dupattas*. The waitresses seemed delighted, paraded around in the flowing garments with the gold embroidered *dupattas* draped around shoulders. Sara, the waitress with freckles and short red hair, took to wearing her tunic with jeans on the street to and from the restaurant during weekend shifts with the scarf wrapped regally around her shoulders. She admitted that she sometimes wore it while out on Saturday evenings.

Once Mo asked Uncle what "butt" meant, after seeing a commercial on television in which youngsters repeated the phrase "Butt out!" while mashing their fags underfoot. Uncle had pointed to Sara's backside saying how *that* was a butt, fondling the fleshy flanks with his eyes, smacking lascivious lips. Sara often gave Mo peculiar looks, and once, blue eyes bright with interest, asked him about the mysteries of Allah. Such a direct question by a subordinate of high status – a white woman raised in the West where he understood everyone had many assets – made Mo panic, found him tongue-tied. He mumbled something unintelligible. The girl was visibly disappointed. It was then that Mo realized that he was not quite himself in English. He would have to practise making his tongue do the strange tricks to make the Canadian sounds, to be understood. More importantly, he would have to practise getting comfortable with Canadian women. But Mo does not understand them.

They look at him during the lunch buffet offered at the restaurant. His uncle has already told him they will find him erotic – exotic? – "You are blessed by our side of the family's good looks: of course you'll get some attention. These women are attracted to tall men in properly cut suits," he said, picking lint from his nephew's lapel, "since they work on Bay Street."

"Aaah, Bay Street." Mo nodded to his uncle, feigning understanding. People trust a man who understands things, or at least looks as if he understands. His father told him this before Mo's departure from Pakistan. He also warned his son that American women were always falling in love. "They are crazy. Do not get involved. Sex-sex-sex and then *no children*

– very strange. Your mother and I are looking for a suitable match for you right now. The proper family and age, sweet and ripe as a mango, fair as a dove. We will send her to you as soon as you have settled in and can support a family."

Uncle nudged him whenever Helen, the young woman from the insurance agency across the street, came into the restaurant for lunch or dinner. She was particularly friendly to Mo, complimented his cheerful accent, the length of his eyelashes, the whiteness of his teeth. At first he was shocked by her forward manner, even more so by the true yellowness of her hair. When he expressed his fear of the woman with doll's hair from the insurance agency, Uncle laughed with his whole belly, calling him infidel – imbecile? Then the older man leaned over as if to impart great words of wisdom and said simply, "She is white all over, and in some places, *pink*."

Mo gasped, remembering pictures he'd seen once, belonging to chums from school. The idea of the different flesh and pink refinements made his phallus grow large, like a blood sausage. He was surprised and flattered when she asked him to accompany her to a restaurant Friday night, where they would eat some kind of sea creature that, to Mo, sounded like the name of a woman. Tamari? Calamity? Calamari? That was it.

"Do you like seafood?" she asked.

Mo nodded dubiously, leaned over to take her plate.

"Good." Helen covered his hand with hers. "Did you hear about the boy in B.C. who killed himself? It was on the news at noon. The kids at school called him a terrorist because his mother wore a hijab. It's so sad – he was only twelve." She squeezed Mo's hand and her lips pressed together in sympathy.

Mo tells this piece of news to Uncle and Aunty once the dinner rush slows down. Uncle heaves a great sigh. He closes the restaurant early that evening, lets Hari, the cook, the porter and the waitresses go, and they all kneel on the Persian carpet facing Mecca, pray as the sun disappears from the sky. Uncle and Aunty shake their heads, leave the restaurant after Mo offers to check the stock for tomorrow and take care of the cash and float. He puts on one of the CDs Uncle bought during his last trip to Little India – the latest film soundtrack. He whistles as he counts; coins fall into the deposit bag in time with the beat of the chorus.

After dropping the bag into the bank slot, Mo continues down the street. The streetcar, he decides, will take a long time, and he often feels stifled in the train carriages and the subway stations with their tiled walls – like gigantic bathrooms. Mo hears his dress shoes slap against the pavement. He comes to a nice neighbourhood, where many of the brightly painted houses display flowers and shrubs in the front yards. The scent of jasmine wafts through the street and Mo almost stops in the middle of the sidewalk, remembering the *chambeli* of his mother's garden. He is filled with a sudden wave of longing and thinks about the boy who was bullied at school. He thinks about Yusuf, being held in detention without a lawyer to aid him. This is such a strange place: bounteous, wonderful, cruel.

Mo turns the corner to find an older gent in an overcoat loping along the street. He turns suddenly and in the light of the streetlamp, Mo sees the man smile at him. Mo is caught off guard, but manages to smile back. He remembers the pre-lunch newsflash last year; the American journalist being decapitated on television. He remembers turning the TV on at the restaurant, thankfully, before the crowd arrived. Suddenly there was a horrifying scene of a man having his head removed by a blade. A second later, the weather report flickered across the screen. Mo had forced himself to lift the remote, turn off the TV and go to the washroom where he found he couldn't stop shaking. He'd kept wanting to throw up in the sink, but nothing would come out.

All throughout the day he'd felt a mild nausea and a deep confusion at what the hooded men were trying to do. They were called Islamic extremists and terrorists. Now everyone was afraid and confused – especially Mo. He feared people would automatically associate any Muslim with evil. But he couldn't help wondering a few things: did the hooded men have a legitimate quarrel? How many wars had there been in the Middle East? And what was it that tied blood, oil and power together, and did this rely on religious belief or was that also some kind of mask, or hood?

The tree branches sway in the night breeze and Mo looks around the neighbourhood, sees the warm glow in people's windows as they go about their business watching television, reading, playing with their children. He gulps the fresh night air in the deserted street. He feels a calmness he remembers from when he was a child. Waking early, before anyone else in the household, he would open the window and survey the sky, the sun peeking over the horizon, and the peace of the morning would make his eyes water with a strange joy. There would be just a slip of fragrance from the jasmine before it closed itself for sleep during the day. Mo considers the unexpected beauty and brutality of the world, that these two forces exist together, side by side. He feels a dull ache in his chest, pushes his hands into his trouser pockets and walks all the way home.

On Friday evening, Helen meets Mo at his uncle's restaurant. Her hair is windblown back from her face in two large feathery curls. "I'm sooo relaxed now. Just went out with some of the colleagues for a few drinks, and Chardonnay always puts me in a very good mood." Her eyes sparkle.

Mo is unsure how he feels about her having consumed alcohol, especially on a Friday. But he knows that a drink before the weekend is an important aspect of being Canadian and decides he will partake of this wine ritual at dinner.

As Helen drives into the parking lot beside the restaurant, a black sports car pulls up so close to them they can hear the music pounding from the vehicle. Suddenly the rear window opens and a large set of pasty buttocks bulges out.

"Butt out!" shouts Mo, pointing at the downy cheeks. "Now I get it. People are so in love with the bum in this country. No wonder homosexuals have such power!"

Helen can't look away from the horror of the full moon in the parking lot. She grabs Mo's hand, pulls him away.

Minutes later, a waiter dressed in a white shirt and black

trousers brings Helen and Mo a platter each of the calamari animal Helen has been talking about, with a serving of rice and grilled vegetables. Mo chews the rubbery creatures. He silently counts the number of them left on his plate, and smiles at the smiling woman sitting across from him. An idea seizes Mo that makes him want to spit it out, and he does so, discreetly, into his napkin.

"The creature makes an argument in my belly," he says, grimacing. "It is not agreeing with me." The fried calamari seemed to him like the elastic ring of an anus: perhaps of a cat or dog? How easily this restaurant fools the unthinking Canadian people. He wonders if it might be rude to tell Helen that right now she was probably eating the sphincters of various animals. Mo twirls the leaves of lettuce from his plate on his fork, letting the salad dressing drip and decides not to mention it. He stares in fascination as she eats happily, taking long sips of wine from her goblet, giving him looks that make him uncomfortable in the pants. Mo finishes his serving of vegetables, his sweet salad and salty rice.

Outside the restaurant, Helen takes his hand. Unfamiliar with this kind of display of affection, Mo smiles, stiffly swings their hands back and forth as they walk along the street, heading to the parking lot. Once there, they are greeted by the ruckus of a group of boys leaning against that same black sports car parked next to Helen's. The boys argue boisterously and smoke cigarettes. Two of them are engaged in a wrestling match on the pavement. The one in a baseball cap takes long drags of his cigarette.

"Hey, Paki."

"Hey, stinky Paki."

"Go back home, Paki."

Helen clutches Mo's hand tightly. Mo is used to this sort of thing, although he wondered at first how these Canadian people would know the word *Pak* meant clean and pure – holy – in his language. He understood then that it was really true, what the commercials on television said about multiculturalism. The addition of the diminutive form, *turning*

'John' to 'Johnny' – he heard one of his past teachers explain – made their attempt at friendliness that much more endearing. His translation abilities of common expressions needed more practice, but he understands the essence of what the fellows mean:

Hello, perfect friend.

You carry such a pure fragrance.

Safe return to your holiest of homes.

Mo repeats the boys' greetings the way he always returned them – not wanting to be impolite – with a wide, friendly smile.

The young men look puzzled, glance at each other uncomfortably. The wrestlers stop for a moment. The smoker shrugs, takes a few short puffs of his cigarette and punches one of his friends on the arm.

Mo pulls Helen along to her side of the car and opens the door for her. She looks at him mournfully, wobbling on her high heels. "I am soo sorry."

"It is perfectly fine, I will be better tomorrow," Mo says, patting his belly, assuming she's apologizing for his calamari stomach ache. He helps her into the driver's seat, and walks around to the other side.

When Helen leans toward him in the car, the neck of her blouse falls open slightly, so that Mo can see how white white really is. Her cheeks are soft, her breath is warm on his face as she gives him a drunken hug. He touches the blonde strands of hair near her ear, carefully. They are softer than he imagined and he feels as if he's touching some rarely seen creature, like those he reads about in the simpler passages of wildlife magazines. She is very pretty – more than that. When he looks in her eyes, he sees the gentleness of perhaps a ... doe.

When she drops him off, he cannot bring himself to kiss her as she desires – on the lips. Considering what has been in her mouth in the course of the evening, Mo gives her an affable peck on the cheek instead.

The next day, Mo decides he will put up a sign in the window of the restaurant. He is just about to paste it on the glass when Ahmed stops him. Nodding his head, the older man says in their language, "Yes, yes, I know what you mean, but I believe this would be more appropriate," he carefully paints whiteout over the last word of the sign – sphincter. He prints the correct word over it.

"How is it you and I know, but these people cannot figure it out?" asks Mo. He takes his time, measuring dimensions to make sure the sign is straight then goes out onto the street, to see how it looks beside the menu and the stickers displaying acceptable credit cards – a white placard with words written in thick, black marker: In this restaurant we do not serve assholes.

"You can't have a sign like that in the window!" says Aunty when she arrives, hours later. "It will ruin business."

"Keep it! Keep it!" the waitresses plead.

"Hey, Iqbal. Great sign!" says one of the customers as he leads a group of laughing co-workers to their usual table.

Uncle raises a brow at Aunty. "What sign?"

Just then Aunty's friend, Muneera, comes through the glass door. "*Arragh!* Your sign is very gutsy, Iqbal. I wouldn't have expected it."

"Well, I can't take the credit. It was Mo's idea."

Muneera eyes Mo. "Well, not just a handsome face! Listen," she lowers her voice and the lines of her forehead deepen as she leans into the counter. "They are deporting Yusuf. Without any kind of explanation. He still has another year left on his student visa!"

Mo knows the story: Yusuf was arrested in the middle of the night. They never told him what the charges were. It was like some strange film about the Second World War. Mo met Yusuf at an Eid celebration held at the mosque last year. The young man appeared average in every way, but it seemed anyone from Pakistan was under suspicion. Could he have been involved in anything? Mo didn't know his family or anything about him, except that he'd been in the country for two years and was studying at one of the universities downtown. The police had never given any evidence against him, or a reason for why it was necessary for him to be in jail.

"I told his mother before he left, *Let him come – we will take care of him.* But how? There are no laws for him!" Muneera cries.

Aunty puts an arm around the woman. "We will stand together on this and write letters and make phone calls. These people are not unreasonable."

The dining room is already filling up with the lunch crowd and waitresses float by like butterflies in their gauzy outfits. Muneera starts weeping into her shawl.

"Now, now," Aunty says to her, then she gestures to Mo and whispers, "Go fetch a box of sweets."

Mo picks out the best unbroken pieces of burfi and ladoos, places them in a small box lined with wax paper and seals it with a piece of tape.

"Thank you, sister," Muneera opens the box and bites into one of the sweets right away. "Oh, so good. No point in dieting anymore, not since the arrest, anyway." She moves to the exit. "*Salaam aleikum!*" she says as she pushes the glass door open.

"*Aleikum salaam,*" calls Aunty. Peace be unto you.

That night Mo once again offers to close the restaurant by himself. He likes having some time away from Uncle and Aunty and their cool, almost arrogant children at home. The boys speak a language he does not fully comprehend, and usually socialize in front of the television or video game screen. "Dude! Beat your score!" He often hears them yelling from the kitchen.

Mo decides to walk home again, so that he might witness the kind of domestic happiness, so carefree, that people seem to enjoy in this country – their lives filled with ease and opportunity. Or is it an illusion? As he strolls through the dark downtown neighbourhood, the night breeze rustles the leaves of the tall maples around him. He tries to sink into the calm he felt that night when he saw the man in the overcoat, remembered that quiet, mysterious joy from his childhood – but the effort is too taxing. He can't stop the thoughts racing in his mind like wild dogs. They have already taken something from you if you only feel fear, he thinks. It makes him angry. His pace quickens and he can hear the hard clack of his dress shoes on the sidewalk.

Then all at once he catches the smell of *chambeli*. Jasmine. He stops, feels his shoulders drop. The night opens to him. Mo is hesitant to take a step and leave the scent behind, but he continues slowly, hands in his pockets. He whistles the Bollywood soundtrack tune from the restaurant. An idea strikes him. *Tomorrow, I will tell them to call me by my name.* Whistling even louder, Mohamed makes his way home.

THE HOUSE ACROSS THE WAY

It was on my second Saturday in Leerdam that I first heard of Uncle Kumar's son, Vishnu. I was looking out on the tropical morning from the balcony, watching the sun dazzle the blue, expansive sea when Asra stepped near the railing. I scooped her up, spun around until she started laughing and shrieking. When I put her down, she pulled at the frilled hem of her nightie, suddenly shy again with her new Aunty. Her excited cry had caused a neighbour on the road to look up, wave and call "Hello, Asra!"

Instantly, Uncle Kumar's macaw with the long blue, yellow and red clipped wings repeated: "Asra! Asra!" It did this whenever anyone called the beloved girl.

I heard my cousin's laugh from inside; then she appeared at the doorway wiping her hands on a kitchen towel. Rashida told me that the first time she heard the macaw – the name of her daughter repeated in that way – it was only a few days after the funeral and she'd wept for hours while her husband was at work; she'd cleaned the pots and pans, her tears dripping into the washtub full of dirty dishes, into the soapy clothes soaking in the plastic basin at the pipe and drain of the bottomhouse, into the stew cooking on the stove – her face wet and eyes shining all day.

"Just so," Rashida explained, "Vishnu shouted for Asra when he came back from the rice field. Sometimes he would just pull her onto the tractor and off they'd go until the afternoon! And how that macaw call ... with the same voice, like he still deh with us." She shook her head in disbelief, adding that sometimes she had to check that Vishnu wasn't standing out on the road, waiting for a sign of her daughter. He appeared in her dreams and they talked – the way she had conversations with many people who were gone – but with him, when she realized that he was dead, she wasn't afraid the way she was with others. "Like he sitting in the kitchen with me having some *poloughrie* and pepper sauce, taking a beer," Rashida said. She disappeared into the house and returned holding a photograph.

"Here's a picture of Vishnu last year after harvest, with his brother Arjun." She placed it in my lap and my eyes immediately caught the image of the young man I'd seen recently, in the yard of the house across the way.

"Look how handsome he was," she pointed to Vishnu. The brothers stood in front of the sea wall. "So tall, with such a bright smile, like Uncle Kumar in his younger days. Oh plenty girls liked Vish ... but he only wanted one." She nudged me. "And she was the wrong one, according to his parents." But I was busy studying Arjun's smaller frame, his laughing face and green eyes flashing at the camera, a long cowlick of hair falling into one eye.

The week earlier Asra had pulled me onto the road toward the seawall, excited about showing me the Leerdam beach. The sun had started its long descent into the ocean and it was only at this time, a few hours before dusk, that anyone ventured from the shade in the village.

We walked toward Uncle Kumar's house, where I noticed a gathering of young men in the yard. They were drinking beer, telling stories and jokes – their jeers and laughter echoing along the narrow corridor of houses. With Asra's little hand in mine, we walked nearer to the crowd. Their eyes turned toward me, and I felt the silence that occurs when a woman passes a group of men. I expected a comment – a witty come-on, a fresh Caribbean quip – but they remained quiet, uncomfortable, and I dared to look at them only to meet fleeing eyes, furtive sips of beer, distracted fiddling.

Then I noticed one brown face, eyes glinting green and meeting mine in a direct and somewhat curious way. He wasn't hidden under the long cowlick as in his photograph; his head was shaved except for a small ceremonial ponytail in back, the *churki* he'd worn since his brother's funeral. The amusement in his gaze made me turn away suddenly and I thought I felt him smile.

When I'd first arrived, so much of the newness of Guyana had passed in a blur. The first dreamlike memory was my nighttime arrival at Cheddi Jagan Airport. Before the images of the village came the sensate jumble of the tropical sea-salt air, the blackness of the road at night, the towering coconut trees guarding each house in every neighbourhood.

I remember the first time I saw Uncle Kumar's son, Arjun, because from that day forward, I looked for him. In my cousin's high balcony facing the sea, from my position with a book in my hands, my hammock barely swinging, I sometimes watched the way he gracefully mounted his bicycle to go work on his father's rice farm: there was the solemnity of his face, the grief that framed his body. If he saw me hanging clothes in the bottomhouse or playing with the children in the road, he'd wave with a smile. I greeted him inconsistently: an eager wave and friendly smile, or a taciturn 'Hi', in a cool manner. Was it forward of me to be friendly? Or was I supposed to be coy, ignoring him at every chance, except when he least expected it, like the girls in the Indian films I'd seen – the ones that my mother's generation grew up watching.

I'd handed the photo back to Rashida and nestled into the hammock, picking up the Henry James novel I'd brought with me.

I noticed Uncle Kumar's wife walking on the dirt road with a large basket of fruits to be sold at the local market. I stared, mystified by the ease with which she weaved through the streets with the basket balanced perfectly on her head.

A few minutes later, there was Arjun, sitting in the hammock of his bottomhouse, talking to a girl seated on the bench beside him.

Rashida sent me to fetch Asra, who by that time was making her rounds at the neighbours' houses. I heard giggling, and found Asra sitting with a boy, both of them devouring mangoes from a pile of fruit underneath the mango tree in the yard. "Aunty Meea, come – watch how much mango deh here!" Asra squealed when she spotted me.

"How many you eat already?" I asked with mock concern, trying to speak the local dialect, since she couldn't understand me otherwise. "You know what happen when you have too much mango ..." I warned, enjoying the wide-eyed attention of both children. "You start to grow hairy teeth!"

"Fi true?" gasped Asra, turning to her friend with an incredulous look.

"Come, le' we go before it start." I took her hand and she waved goodbye to the boy. As we headed back to our house, someone called, "Like Asra get a new friend!" It was the young woman in Arjun's yard.

"Aunty!" shouted Asra, breaking from me and running toward her. Although the woman was partially covered by the shade, I could make out a beckoning arm. "You're from outside, aren't you? I can tell from the way you walk." She eyed me up and down, then asked almost suspiciously, "Canada or America?"

"Canada."

"Girl, you from one cold place!"

I laughed. My eyes strayed to Arjun, who lay in the hammock as if he'd never seen me before.

"Yes, all the Guyanese from outside come back for the sun ... or to get married."

She gave me a knowing look. I almost expected a wink.

"Oh, but I'm too young for marriage," I said, winking at her instead, knowing that in this part of the world I was already in danger of spinsterhood. It would be inconceivable to her, my cousin, or anyone here that, even with my tall, boyish figure, pixie haircut, and modern values, I might even be able to wait 'til I was thirty before getting married in a place like Canada. I waved goodbye and Asra ran ahead, climbing deftly up the staircase with hands and knees and feet.

When I offered to make dinner that evening, Rashida kissed her teeth. "Not unless you know how to make bake and saltfish the way Haroun like it." She laughed off the suggestion, then asked if I wouldn't mind getting some ice cream instead.

I hurried out before Rashida started setting the table, knowing the neighbourhood stores would close early. At night the village was another place; there were very few people on the road except for commuters coming home from their jobs in Georgetown.

The nearest shop was dark, its entrance gate padlocked. I could hear the family inside having a meal in the living quarters of the house – plates and cutlery clinked while voices mingled over the noise of a television. I had to watch my step on the dirt road, barely able to negotiate the tracks in the mud from large tractor wheels, human and animal footprints. On the main road a lonely streetlamp burned, casting long-figured shadows. The big shop's lights were still on and I was relieved to find a few small cartons of ice cream from the tiny freezer and be back on my way to the house.

Looking down the smaller roads, I could barely see the towering palms though I heard their leaves swishing. I hurried along in the darkness, startled by a sudden cow grazing by the roadside. Men in billowing white shirts careened through the darkness on bicycles, and dogs hopped along, ownerless, on the village road.

The street Rashida lived on was empty, except for a young man striding towards the sea wall. The breeze blew through his open shirt as he turned to look at me. For a second I saw a face that looked familiar, that I couldn't quite place – then he turned and continued to the wall. It wasn't until I was climbing the steps of the house that a shudder went through me as I realized the man I'd seen was Vishnu.

In the indigo dawn, the roosters heralded the new day with long guttural calls. The sun appeared just after that, burning layers of gold and purple in the sky. Rashida had spent the early morning preparing for an outing to the beach. There was cook-up rice in the pot, bags of ice from the freezer ready to go in the cooler with the beer and soda, and chicken locked in a plastic container. She was packing everything into the large straw market bag when I woke up.

"Don't worry with your shower so early," she said, noticing my zombie-like trek to the shower stall, "you hardly get a chance to sweat yet!" She was accustomed to my usual routine, which, by the end of the day, added up to at least three cold showers, if there was an ample supply of water and no blackouts. My cousin washed her hands, disappeared into her bedroom and was ready to go in five minutes.

When I finally ran down the steps with my gear and camera, I found everyone waiting in the minibus that Haroun usually drove on a small stretch of the Parika-Vreed-en-Hoop route: a part of the transnational road that went from the Suriname border and continued on the other side of the Essequibo River to Venezuela. Asra played with a beach ball in the back seat and Rashida sat in front of her with all of the food piled into the seat beside her. Wearing a green baseball cap, Haroun sat in the front seat beside Arjun.

Haroun started the engine and we pulled onto the narrow street, heading for Parika. My interest immediately fixed on the streets and villages that flew past the window: the old women in granny dresses, both young and older boys in short pants on bicycles *liming* at the shops and Chinese restaurants. The few women I saw who weren't hanging clothes on a line in their yards walked briskly, in a business-like way on the road, clutching purses as they waited to catch a bus either towards the market or Georgetown.

We slowed at Parika, passing the long strip of vendor stalls and the small port from which ferries traveled to the Essequibo Islands and into the interior to former Arawak and Wapashimi territories. I grabbed one of the bags with food and followed Rashida and the family from the brush of a makeshift parking lot up a grassy incline. There lay the sandy beach and brown shore, the dark water lapping invitingly. We walked past a group of tourists or VSO workers laughing and drinking beer on a blanket, and settled near the shade of a few bamboo trees.

Rashida started unpacking the food and promptly took out portions for everyone. Haroun and Arjun ate quickly and left us on the blanket. I saw that they were headed to a group of teenaged boys and girls playing cricket farther down the beach.

When my cousin finished feeding Asra, she joined me in the shade with a sigh and we ate our lunch, watching the rolling of the waves. Rashida joked about walking over to the cricket players, where I might spot a nice mango to take back with me to Canada. The kind of mango who might be ripe for marriage. The next thing I knew, she was off in the water chasing after Asra.

I pulled my hat over my eyes and leaned back on the blanket, lulled into a peaceful slumber by the ocean and the sounds of laughter and splashing. Then someone tickled my feet. I pulled back my hat and sat up quickly, stunned by the sun.

"You'll take a beer with me?" asked Arjun, dropping a white feather at my toes. He reached into the cooler next to me and pulled out a bottle of Carib, smiling easily. His slow eyes betrayed that he'd already had a drink or two.

"Sure, I'll have one," I said, still a little groggy.

"Sorry I woke you like that. Sometimes I like to play wicked." He placed the wet bottle in my hand. I noticed that he was taking great pains to not speak the regional patois. He sounded like a starched schoolmaster when he asked: "How are you enjoying your stay here?"

"Everything's so different," I said, unable to find even the beginning of a way to compare my tropical surroundings to the cityscape I'd lived in most of my life. "It's beautiful here, the ocean, the trees – the sun is extraordinary."

"Yes, that's what everybody say: Guyana sure hot." He started walking into the shallow water. "Come, you stay cool like this."

Arjun stood in a deeper area and took a swig of beer. His shorts rose up to his waist in the water and I giggled, pointing. He looked embarrassed for an instant and pushed the bloated material into the water, then laughed as it rose once again.

I waded into the cold water slowly, standing beside him while he looked thoughtfully, smiling at the horizon. "You think you could settle in a place like this?" he asked.

"I don't know. I'm really just on holiday, but maybe I'll stay a while." I sipped my beer, considering this new option.

He took a long swig, finishing half the bottle, then blurted, "I was thinking about taking you into town one night."

"That would be fun! I haven't been in Georgetown after dark yet." I was excited, aware that the city had a reputation for being dangerous at night.

"I know some nice places there." He took his hat off and ran a hand over the short stubble of his scalp, his fingers lingering where the ceremonial ponytail had once been. "I wasn't always at home like I am now. Last year at this time I was going to the institute in town every day for mechanical studies. Vishnu was the one who took care of the farm with my father. He knew all about it."

My gaze caught the feather on the blanket on the beach. I was suddenly uncomfortable at the mention of his brother's name.

"Since the night he died, everything changed." Arjun looked out at the water.

"It must have been hard for you," I said, trying to find something more adequate, more comforting.

"It's not a long time ago it happened. He was the person I talked to the most out of everyone." Arjun's eyes filled and he chuckled. "Sometimes I'll be in the rice field, just working, then there'll be tears streaming down my face, big long tears on my cheeks from nowhere." His eyes searched the horizon as if he were looking for the shape of his brother in the clouds. He finished his beer. I could see goosebumps rising on his brown skin with the slow breeze that came in from the ocean, and the water beads that clung to his chest and arms fell with the small, sudden shivers that ran along his body.

I reached out to touch his arm. Arjun looked at me and smiled, then pushed his upfloating shorts back into the water so that we could both laugh. He stretched an arm out to the sandy bank and exchanged his empty beer bottle for a rubber ball nestled into the sand. "Come, le' we play a game." He lunged forward into the water.

Haroun noticed the ball being whipped back and forth between us and left the family splashing near the shore to join us. Soon everyone was part of the game, separated into teams, splashing toward the ball while Haroun entertained us with renditions of Radio Guyana calypso and chutney songs.

Arjun beckoned me to leave the group and walk with him. Rashida gave me a smile and yelled, "Watch yourself, girl!" I heard her laughter trailing off behind us.

We walked along the white sand, talking about what it was like to live in the countryside – how different it was from life in Georgetown. When I saw that we were coming to a greener area of secluded brush I turned abruptly and faced him. "Won't your girlfriend hear about it if we're away for too long?" I asked.

"I don't care what she thinks," Arjun answered calmly. "I don't love her." He picked up a bleached-out branch and poked the ground, then turned to me: "Do you think you could love someone from over here?"

"I don't know." I looked at him quizzically.

"What if I told you I already loved you?" He concentrated on the movements of the stick as he poked at tufts of grass.

My skin flushed with a heat warmer than the tropical air. "I would say that's impossible because you don't even know me." My own words sounded unconvincing.

"But if I knew you from the kind of things Rashida and Haroun said about you ..."

I could only smile back. I was flattered, then caught myself. Of course people would discuss any visitor they were entertaining from abroad. We walked past the brush until we reached the part of Parika beach where a DJ was set up and vendors sold coconut water, rum and beer from small roadside huts.

In the company of people once again, we lost our seriousness and stood at the periphery of the bar. Arjun offered to buy a rum and coconut for us both. Before he returned, a few people approached me; as soon as they heard my accent, they chatted me into conversation after conversation.

Arjun and I didn't have a chance to speak in private again, but I felt his eyes on me, hot, watching my every gesture with strangers who bought me drink after drink, until I noticed he'd left the bar.

I excused myself and searched the crowd, found him brooding by the shore, looking out into the horizon the way I did each morning. Arjun turned to me as I walked into the waves beside him and I saw that his eyes were shining. He held out his hand, which I squeezed reassuringly. We waded through the water in silence.

In the van, the sun glowed pink as it sank into the water; the villages tore away from the windows as we sped back to Leerdam. Asra prattled away, her innocent voice breaking into song phrases about "sexybody girls" and heartache, making Arjun and me laugh as we sat in the back seat, quiet and sleepy, knees touching.

When we returned to the house, Rashida put Asra to bed immediately. Haroun took a shower and was soon in the hammock, fast asleep. Rashida yawned, dipping a large cup of potable water from a small covered barrel near the fridge and pouring it into the kettle.

"What happen with Arjun?" she whispered, her eyes wide with interest as she plugged in the kettle for tea. Without giving me a chance to respond, she said, "His friends keep him drinking and sporting so he'll forget, but it doesn't show if it working at all ..."

"What happened to his brother?" I asked.

That started my cousin on the story about Uncle Kumar wanting to arrange a suitable match for his son, the boy everyone looked up to in the village. "Vishnu was good, kind, a nice boy, always helping out in the rice field. He was the son Uncle Kumar wanted to look after the place. But the man wanted the right woman to help his son manage all of the farms ... They have a few pieces of land and money, although you wouldn't know by the way they live ... You see, Uncle Kumar knew that already his son was giving sweet sweet looks to one of the girls who lived by the field. Vish told Haroun one long story about a time he saw the most beautiful girl he ever see picking breadfruit from a tree in her yard, and how the girl waved to him. He passed every day in his tractor and saw her hanging out clothes or cooking up in the bottomhouse or doing some chore after school. She was maybe seventeen, he was only twenty-one. Sometimes she would bring him something sweet – mithai, halwa – or lunch – curry and roti – and hear na, the girl would put flower petals 'pon the plate!"

The kettle whistled and Rashida stood to pour the water into a teapot, adding milk and sugar right away.

"Vish always had a smile on his face when he talked about her. Soon the boy began to call on her at home. Her family, of course, knew all about Uncle Kumar's son. They welcomed Vishnu. In all their dreams they never expect their daughter coulda have a chance of marrying so high up. The lovers went to the movies. Everyone in the village knew something was going on ... even Uncle Kumar and his wife talking that it nice for Vishnu to have fun and friends, but that some day he would have to respect tradition and his parents' wishes. A day Vishnu come home and announced his plan to get engaged to the village girl, and Uncle Kumar take off he belt and thrash the boy and cuff him up, and poor Vish couldn't raise he hand against the old man. See how good he was? Meena get the tea, na?"

I did as my cousin asked and pulled two cups from the cupboard, checking for ants before pouring out tea for both of us.

"Good." She took the cup from me. "Uncle Kumar threatened Vish, saying that if he marry this girl he'll never speak to him again ... and not a penny, not an acre from any of the farms. All night, every day the two boys – you know

Vish and Haroun were like brothers – would be discussing this thing at the Chinese restaurant or the rum shop."

Rashida finished her tea. "Sometimes the boy would come back with Haroun so drunk, so vex with Uncle Kumar, he'd end up sleeping right here, in the same room that you're in."

I sat up bolt straight in my chair, alarmed. The look on my face made my cousin smile. Icy fingers played up my spine.

Rashida stood up and gathered our empty teacups, placed the dirty dishes in the sink. She looked at the clock. "Oh gosh! Past ten o'clock already," while she hurried to her bedroom. "We'll finish tomorrow," she whispered.

"Watch how late you hens gaffing away," I heard Haroun mutter irritably. He kissed his teeth; then there was silence in the house.

I walked to the fastened balcony doors and peered into the darkness. There was only the low-hanging moon and its reflection on the calm ocean waves. The village street was quiet except for the bark of a dog engaged in a short dialogue with a dog from the neighbouring village, blocks away.

Tomorrow there would be a bit of excitement, since Uncle Kumar was returning from a Caricom developmental conference in Jamaica. He was due to arrive very early the day after next, and Haroun had agreed to pick him up at the airport with Arjun, for extra protection against robbers.

I looked towards the house across the way and saw a figure carefully creeping down the stairs, then spotted another person outlined by moon-glow, coming down the road towards the house. It was Arjun's girlfriend. I could tell from the roundness of her figure, the jaunt of her walk. She was meeting him tonight – this was the appointed time. My heart skipped a beat when I saw him close his gate and put his arm around her, the two lovers walking on the road towards the beach.

I felt a mild shock, though it shouldn't have surprised me. I had an urge to open the balcony doors and yell his name into the street just so he'd know that I saw him, but it would've been pointless. My restlessness was replaced by a surprising lassitude. I sighed, turning off the lights and went to bed, listening to wave after wave lashing the seawall. I dreamed of the ocean and people I didn't recognize drifted in and out of the dream. Asra asked me to take her to the beach and I woke with the cock's crow, just before five o'clock.

All day I waited for Rashida's cue to sit down so that she could finish the story. It finally came after dinner when Haroun retired in order to rest up for the early morning airport pick-up. My cousin gathered Asra in her arms; the child had fallen asleep in front of the television set once again. As soon as Rashida turned off the television, the thick weave of sound made by the crickets outside poured into the living room.

"Let we finish this story one time," she said, a flicker of excitement in her eyes as she pulled a pair of pants from the back of a kitchen chair, took a needle and thread from a box inside a hidden compartment of the coffee table, and joined me on the settee where I was flipping through one of the women's magazines I'd brought for her from Canada. She threaded the needle and began hemming up the pants.

"After that night of trouble between Uncle Kumar and the boy about the engagement, the old man forbid meetings between his son and the girl. He went straight to the girl's parents to explain the situation ... that Vishnu already promised to someone else ... though he tellin' a lie. One night Vishnu came back home late late, after taking the girl to a restaurant in town. Uncle Kumar get so vex with the boy he give him some good licks with the belt. The neighbours hear the two quarrel ... shouting, the noise of all type of bric-a-brac being thrashed, broken glass, Uncle Kumar's wife yelling and crying. The next thing, Vishnu standing in front of the house sucking on a bottle of rum, calling Haroun down to the bottomhouse. Well, Haroun go down and drink with him, then Vishnu left, saying how he going to fetch Arjun. Half an hour later there was one set of noise coming from the house, like the old lady being attacked. Arjun run to the bottomhouse and call Haroun to take Vishnu to the hospital because he drank poison. He say the boy choking like he ready to bring up, but nothing coming. All of we wait at the hospital the whole night ... the old lady and Uncle Kumar crying steady steady, me and Haroun watching, waiting and Arjun walking the whole hospital ... quiet, dry-eyed. Once, after an hour or so, the nurse come out to say that it maybe too late for any of the medicines to work. Before the sun rise the next day, the doctor tell us Vishnu gone."

Rashida seemed fatigued by the details and let out a long sigh. "A day the next week Uncle Kumar get a letter in the mailbox with just one line written: *You killed your own son.* But hear na," she looked up from her sewing, "nobody sign it."

She held up the pair of pants and checked the straightness and strength of the stitches by briskly pulling the pant leg across the seam. She rose from her seat on the couch slowly, like a much older woman, and asked me to lock up the house properly before going to sleep. "I definitely ready to catch my bed," she yawned, stretching.

I, on the other hand, was as alert as a chicken loose from the yard. I turned the deadbolts and latches for both entrances and headed for the hammock on the balcony, staring at the dark sky and sea.

The black water rose and fell, shifting like a beast. My skin prickled with shudders of wind sweeping up from the sea wall. Everything that was familiar lay across an entire ocean, halfway across the continent. In that place, it was possible to choose any path for your life, but it was unreachable from here. Even though the whole world, which seemed endless in the dark, opened its arms to me, I felt enclosed – as if a veil separated my prior life from the reality I suddenly faced.

I went inside to the living room and reached for the television remote, knowing that one of the national stations picked up American channels via satellite. I flipped from an episode of *M*A*S*H* to MTV, then watched the Discovery Channel and finally settled on a bad late-night feature film. Although my eyes burned, I kept myself up and watching. The clock chimed four times although it was only one o'clock when the film ended, and I swayed dizzily as I stood up and realized once more where I was.

Two small geckos clung to the ceiling, near the light, where the hunt for insects was best. As I brushed my teeth in the sink, a small translucent frog climbed out from the mouth of the drain and I jumped back. It sat calmly in the basin, watching me.

I turned out the lights and felt my way to my bedroom in the back of the house quickly, heart racing, still unaccustomed to the blackness of a rural night in the tropics.

I crawled under the netting, and lay in bed, tired, yet awake. Fear sank into me like an anchor: the black air was suffocating, the netting felt like a shroud, and I had to pull it up quickly to breathe, forgetting the hot sting of evening mosquitoes, and the cockroaches that might be skittering on the floor.

I jumped out of the bed, almost bounding across the room, and opened the jalousie window to get some air. I felt I was being propelled into a great void and wanted to throw open the bolted doors, to run to the seawall, to breathe in the ocean air. I needed to feel freedom and escape this terrible sadness. But I knew I couldn't head out into the streets, since only bad things stirred at night; thieves and drunkards who wouldn't think twice about cutting or killing you for a watch, jewellery, a wallet. *This country lawless*, Rashida had said. And it was true: this place was governed by rules I couldn't understand. These people lived, struggled and died silently, invisibly. And now here I was, shipwrecked with them – these people – my family.

I poured a glass of cold water and drank slowly, needing the cool to transform the heat as thick and impenetrable as darkness. I went back to bed and tucked the netting under the mattress once again.

While I was listening to the whir of the oscillating fan and the rolling of the sea washing in and out, the room swirled and collapsed around me and I fell into the depths of dreamsleep. I saw Arjun's face – he was whispering something. I stepped closer to hear him better, but he kept walking backwards into the water at the beach.

My body convulsed awake, and the fluttering of a man's white shirt in a breeze came through the window. But it was only the curtain. The palms outside swished with the breath of the sea. The house was silent, save for a mosquito buzzing in futility, trying to find a hole in the net. Then I was at the beach again, in the dark with Arjun. He was holding my hand as we swam in the ink-black water, moving farther and farther away from the shore. I could taste the salt of the ocean on my tongue.

"Haroun," someone called. My heart pounded awake. It was pitch black and no one responded, everyone too deep asleep to hear the voice. "Haroun," the voice rasped again. The hairs on my neck and arms rose – nobody in the house stirred. The voice came from my window.

Then there came a loud shout from a voice I recognized as Arjun's. Haroun rolled in his bed and grumbled.

"Haroun, wake na man," Arjun called a second time.

"I comin' just now!" yelled Haroun.

Footsteps moved across the kitchen floor as Rashida scuttled about to warm up food and make tea for her husband. There were pots and pans clattering and soon the smell of green mango in fish curry permeated the house. My eyes closed again and the early morning darkness spilled into my dream of a road leading to the airport. Arjun and Haroun were in the front of the van on the way to the airport to pick up Uncle Kumar, but somehow the old man was already in the van with his suitcase. I was confused to see Vishnu sitting placidly beside him, an arm dangling loosely around his father's shoulders.

"Haroun!" The prickly voice penetrated the edges of my dream. The van disappeared into the brightness of the tropical horizon. The next call was low and tortured. My eyes opened. Before the final utterance, the voice became the gravelly crowing of a cock. As the blue glow of morning trembled with dawn's fire, the rooster welcomed the day again, clear and loud. I felt a strange disorienting panic, but steadied myself and listened to the early morning sounds of palm leaves swishing in sea wind. The waves rolling in lulled me into a deep, restless sleep.

There was shouting and crying in the village. I pulled the netting away from my bed and hurried to the balcony where my cousin stood with little Asra sitting astride her hip. Uncle Kumar's wife stood in the street below, sobbing in the arms of one of the neighbourhood women.

Rashida told me that the old woman had just received a telegram saying that her husband had been in an accident on the way to the airport in Kingston, that he'd died in the hospital.

"Whey uncle?" asked Asra.

Rashida tried to answer and stopped. "Uncle gone to Georgetown," her voice cracked.

"He bring me back a nice dress?"

Rashida smiled. "Yes man, a pretty pretty dress."

"Have you seen Arjun?" I asked.

Rashida shook her head.

I was out the door and down the stairs, stepping into my rubber slippers and down the street before she could say anything. I found Arjun rocking in his hammock in the bottomhouse, alone. He turned to me calmly when I opened the gate and stepped into the yard.

"Arjun, I'm sorry …" I sat down on a bench beside him.

He was silent, blinked, went back to rocking. I held out my hand to touch his arm.

"You must go back where you belong," he said angrily. He laid one arm across his face for a moment. When he removed it I saw a flash of vulnerability – the same tenderness in his eyes from Parika beach that day – though he wasn't looking at me. His gaze fixed on the clouds and the sky poured into him.

THE HATMAKER

We knew it was a bad name for the hotel. Not evil bad, maybe in poor taste, maybe reflecting my sense of humour, since neither of us is named Bates. What's surprising is that hardly any of the people who stay here seem to get it or comment on it. That's what made Putnam different. "I think it was the Bates Motel, not Hotel, wasn't it?" He'd laughed.

As soon as those guys came up in September, I remember thinking to myself, bad time of year to be up in Iqualuit. God knows most of the workers leave just at the end of November, when the arctic sun appears for only a few hours. By mid-December, there's maybe an hour of light and if it's cloudy, well ... not even that. But he seemed like a good guy for a management type. Heard about him and the crew staying at the government house from Johnson, who picks up spare work from the departments, whoever they might be: fishing, heritage, mining. This time it was heritage: building the new community centre. I remember thinking, these city boys are coming up here for the winter? Was the government crazy? Well ...

They'd stayed here in our hotel for the first week or so in the fall while getting oriented by my husband, Bill. He usually shows the new groups around town, tells them about Nunavut culture and the way the town is organized – how to walk in a squall, where to get outfitted if in need of gear, where's the best ice fishing and dog sledding. Part of our school is also being renovated. Looks like they're giving us an updated gymnasium we can use for community events, and a new library to boot.

So in a few weeks Johnson reports that Mr. Putnam, the foreman, is settled in at the house and he shops at the dry goods counter and even cooks the meals on Mondays and Tuesdays! Usually those boys will just come here each night and get filled up with the dinner special and a few pints. But Johnson says Mr. Putnam cleans and he's also very tidy, so of course the first thing I think is, well ... I mean you can usually tell: a bit more colour in the clothing, or in the way they speak, but some of them don't give anything away until you hear about what they look at on the internet!

"Nope, it's not that," says Johnson. "He's English."

"Like, you mean from Toronto?" I say.

"No, Betty, he's from England."

"Oh, I get it."

And they say he's started buying sculptures from Nat and Tom. Polar bears and ancestral figures and now Nat and Tom are thinking they can pitch a house somewheres if he keeps paying up like that. And he'll even include a glass or two of rye while he looks over the new deal, some inukshuk or seal or polar bear, and Nat and Tom leave all giggly, talking all loud and brash, knowing they're not supposed to be drinking. Funny, 'cause where I come from everyone drinks and is allowed to drink and God knows they'll drink however much for however long they can manage. Native or not.

One day Mr. Putnam comes by the hotel in the afternoon for lunch.

"You alright, Betty?" He sees me sitting at the counter crocheting up a scarf for Bill's sister – a bright red yarn that I picked up on sale from the Bay store in Calgary on my last trip back.

He asks if I can make hats 'cause his head gets pretty cold out there and the one he has is a dull grey colour.

I say sure and he asks how much. Never thought about having someone pay for it before, but why not? That's probably how prostitution started too!

"Could you knit me a black one, with a single red stripe – like the red you've got in your hands right now?"

And I'm thinking, great, now I get to use up the last bits from Cheryl's hat!

So Putnam sits himself down with his newspaper, and partway through his burger, in comes another guy who's staying at the hotel, just checked in the other day and obviously knows him. They nod to each other and the tall guy with shorn hair and a gut, Davis, plonks down at the bar. He orders a double on the rocks and that gets Putnam's attention. Even more when Davis downs the first one like it's water and orders another.

"I think you're still on the clock, Davis. I'm not sure another is such a good idea."

"Well boss, considering it's colder than a witch's tit out there, I think you can overlook this. Why don't you join me?" Davis waves him over, but Putnam looks at him unimpressed and finishes his meal in silence. Just gets up, drops a ten and some change and leaves.

"Guy's got an icicle up his ass," says Davis. "You think he knows what it feels like to not be able to feed your kids?"

"Well, I imagine he saves a lot since he doesn't drink at lunch," is all I say, getting back to my bobble stitch. I don't say anything else 'cause I don't like Davis's attitude much.

That night we hear Davis inviting people up to his room at the hotel late at night. When I enter the corridor on his floor I can hear music, people yelling and beer bottles clinking around. It sounds like a nightclub! I don't knock on the door or say anything, and I even wait 'til I gather enough nerve to burst in with indignation, but after a bit, I just shrug it off. I mention it to Bill instead.

In a couple of days I tell Johnson to give Mr. Putnam a message that his hat's ready.

Johnson smiles and says, "Bill tell you about that dogsled trip we took last week out to the Bay?"

"He said you all took Putnam into the wilderness thinking he'd faint when you shot the elk out there. But he was the first to dig the knife in."

"Seems he's done his share of hunting. You shoulda seen Bill's eyes bugging when Putnam pulled out this sweet hunting knife and helped skin the thing."

"Well, it's like Bill says: we all got a little bit of Indian in us." Johnson laughed at that one, shook his head.

That afternoon Putnam comes in and smiles when he sees the black hat with the red stripe and the earflaps he asked for, sitting on the counter and me hooking away at the scarf again.

"Betty! Nice work, and promptly done," he says.

Service with a smile. I pass the hat to him and he looks pleased, puts it on and I tell him there's a mirror in the bathroom. He's got that goofy city-folk smile and goes and comes back with an even goofier smile and pulls out the cash.

"Paying off the hotel workers, eh?" Davis walks into the room just then.

"Yes indeed. For this fine hat."

"Doesn't take much to please the English, huh?"

Well. I can see Mr. Putnam's not going to get angry. Too much self-control. But all I can think is, good thing he doesn't have his hunting knife.

"It's the simple things that go over most people's heads," says Putnam, smoothing down his hat.

"I'd say there are a couple of simple things with the job that you might want to reconsider."

"If I need the advice of a subcontractor, I'll ask." Putnam looks to be losing his patience. His face is a sudden pink. He looks at his watch, then says, "Betty, can you make me a roast beef sandwich to go?"

"Why, sure can." So I disappear into the kitchen and hurry with the bread slathering and meat slicing and such.

Davis orders the lunch special but I notice he isn't looking at me with his red eyes, he's staring down Putnam. Don't know what had been said while I was gone but it couldn't have been pleasant. Each of them standing off, like two dogs snarling, waiting to see if there should be an attack or retreat.

A week later we wake up to loud music blaring at three o'clock in the morning. It's coming from Davis's room, so Bill goes up and later he tells me Davis was in there with Nat and Tom and some young girls, like, too young. Not only that, but Davis had this big crate that he checked in with him, full of liquor bottles. It was wide open and there was a 48er of Jack almost empty on the television set. Had to kick them out, and he warned Nat and Tom that they oughtta be careful with girls that young – also with Davis.

"But dude gets us anything we need!" Bill mocks Tom, even imitating the slouch and hands in pockets.

"And how do you pay for it?" Bill asked him, hoping to get the hamster in the wheel turning in the kid's brain, but the hamster's all fucked up on Jack Daniels. Then Bill kicked them out.

"I knew it!" I say to Bill. "That guy is bad news. Comes to the bar and has a couple, then goes back to his room and finishes up a bottle – and up all night like some teenager!"

"Well," says Bill. "Thing is, he's brought a bunch of men to the hotel and the government's paying us high season to house them for a month, so it's better to not make too big a deal. I'll fix his wagon," says Bill. But I know what he means is he'll have a talk with Davis.

I see Putnam each Sunday and Friday for lunch, and he's always wearing his new hat with the red stripe.

"I sent a picture with me in it to my daughter – she says I look very hip!" He laughs.

We talk about the news, what's happening with Obama (Bill always fakes redneck and says, "A black in the White House, eek!") and how the school job is coming along.

"Just a few more months now ..."

He looks very tired whenever he says this, and I hate to tell him, but he's been saying this for a couple of months. Johnson says there've been some setbacks – probably related to Davis being hired.

Bill has contacted the right offices to see if we can get him and his crew in some other housing – since they will be here for at least *a few more months.*

"I've had enough of his shenanigans. You know I hear one of them girls that was here that night got knocked up, surprise, surprise. The thing is, she doesn't know which of them, Tom, or Davis, or one of the other guys, is responsible! And each of them deny everything. Like they couldn't see statutory a million miles away. Girl is fourteen years old!"

Standard business. Bill's sister Cheryl had her first son at fifteen and then two others with someone different who eventually left her. Now she's living on mother's allowance and Bill and I have agreed to get her into school if she can do some correspondence courses and pick up some classes she missed from high school. Girls 'round here can be baby machines, and if they never get out, looks like they just stay that way.

I met Bill down in Calgary during the Stampede. I'm not from here and every November I'm as anxious as a goose waiting to migrate. I remember the first year I came up I'd be in tears every weekend and on the phone with one of my girlfriends. Sure, I'd met some of the wives of Bill's buddies – but it wasn't the same. By December we'd started bingo on Friday and poker on Saturday 'cause the total darkness at 3:00 in the afternoon would have me running for cigarette after cigarette even though I quit years ago. Bill would catch me standing outside on the back deck, moaning with the wind, hiding my smokes. I'd look out at the strange designs of the northern lights, awestruck, bleary-eyed.

It's the kind of place that leaves you alone with your thoughts too much, and it gets brutal enough that, if you're not careful, you stop counting your cigarettes, your drinks, the number of phone calls to girlfriends and special astrologers who only give you good news ... until your husband finds out, and well ... that's when I hung up the phone and picked up crochet.

So at this point, me and Bill got a hat and matching scarf for every day of the week. And we got an extra handmade afghan for each room. But I still get out of here for about six weeks, usually just before Christmas so I can celebrate with my family. Bill comes with me, then flies back right away. Cheryl's good about staying here and helping out. Looks good on a resume, plus her kids love it. I get back to the grind middle of February when there's a bit more sun and the idea of spring doesn't seem as impossible. That way Bill gets to miss me and our Valentine's celebrations are, well …

Good thing we're about to break for Christmas. Things up here are getting a little depressing. Putnam came in at lunch and I swear I've never seen a man in his forties look quite this haggard.

"You alright, Betty?" He sits down and asks for a pint with his burger special. I give him a whisky shot to warm up, and he winks before downing it. So we talk and he says he's taking his daughter skiing. His daughter and his ex live just outside of Toronto. He usually stays with them during Christmas, then takes his daughter away on a special trip.

I feel bad for Putnam. Seems like a lonely life – and truthfully, he's not a bad looking guy. A little skinny though, nothing like Bill. Me, I've always gone for stocky types. And what I liked about Bill was that he looked like he was built to stop a train.

Anyway, after the glass of beer, Putnam jokes about how little sunlight there is, and if it's not overcast, he'll turn up the heat and take off his shirt and sit in the window so his skin remembers the sun. Then he finishes his beer, starts laughing again.

"That Davis character always seems to have the cops at his door! Unfortunately, he never gets caught."

"Funny, 'cause natives get pulled into the slammer for any little thing, but you get a white guy in town, and the cops will go out of their way to leave him alone. Actually, that's the way it works in the rest of Canada. But this is Nunavut." I shrugged.

Putnam looked at me funny, like I was telling him who to vote for or something.

But if you marry a First Nations person, you can't be a total idiot about what's happened in this country.

"Well, Betty." Putnam puts on his old grey hat instead of the new one. "I'll be off to the airport in the evening –"

"Hey, what happened to the hat I made ya?"

"Well, quite honestly, I haven't seen it in a couple of days. I hope it isn't lost but probably claimed by a snowbank at this point! I seem to be missing my hunting knife as well. It was my father's, so I'd like it back – I mean … you'll let me know if you hear anything? Anyway, hope you and Bill have a nice holiday."

"Yeah, for sure, I'll see if anything turns up. You enjoy the warmth down south." I winked at him.

He left a big tip with the burger crumbs and empty pint glass. Soon, everyone will be packing up, including me. And Cheryl will move in to help run the place when Bill comes down to Calgary for a few days. Goodbye twenty-hour days of darkness!

Looks like Cheryl and her kids are still loving the Bates Hotel. She says her marks from her last courses are good enough to get into college. She wants to go for legal secretary! I didn't think she was up for more courses, but sometimes all you need are a few hard knocks to make you see straight.

She asks if I heard about the investigation down in Calgary. And I tell her it got covered for about five minutes on the news in Calgary on a Thursday in January, and since then, I've been getting updates from Bill by phone. But truthfully, who wanted to see Davis there again?

Putnam was the one to report him missing when he didn't show up to work for two days in a row. Bill hadn't heard anything from him, since he'd already moved out of the hotel. When Bill told me Davis was missing I figured he got too fucked up some place, fell asleep in a snowbank or something and couldn't make it to work. Guys like that are always looking for and usually finding trouble.

Cheryl says she saw Putnam when he came in for a drink in the evening, which he never does, unless it's with one of the other bosses. It's one of the nights when Davis was missing. Putnam says he's just come out of the police station – poor guy looked exhausted after being questioned. But he didn't want to say anything. She says he looked a mess, which probably means his shirt wasn't tucked in. She said the look in his eyes was desperate.

"Tell me about the boys, Cheryl. I need to think about something else."

So she rambled on about Eli getting the highest score on his math test the other day, and their Inuktitut classes. Putnam knocked back a couple of glasses of scotch and she could tell that neither the TV he kept glancing at nor her stories really had his attention. He got up, said good night and she's only seen him again during the day, perfectly poised and munching on the lunch special.

Cheryl says the fourteen-year-old groupie who got knocked up has an older brother, Matt, who started on a personal mission to get Davis back for the sick things his sister admitted to being a part of. They got her in rehab at a special detention centre. And Tom was all pissed off at Davis for screwing around with Nat and implicating him, though we all know Nat's a big boy now. And Putnam, well …

"He's pretty nice," says Cheryl, which surprises me, since she's been a nun since her youngest was born. Mad at men, I'd say.

"Not my type. But seems like a decent guy. Responsible," I nod.

Cheryl giggles. "Yeah, he came in for lunch a coupla times each week. We talked about our kids. I told him I was applying to some colleges in Ontario and which were the best, and he lit up like the northern lights. 'My daughter's graduating soon, so I can ask her – which programs are you interested in?' Anyways he was very nice about it and brought me all of this information. A stack yea big of legal assistant and secretary program stuff he'd printed out, and scholarship applications – for mature students and First Nations people. I was surprised he'd gone outta his way so much, but he seemed to want to help out."

"Wow," I say. And I'm thinking to myself, who woulda expected ... but it might work out.

In the end it looks like the cops rounded up all the suspects: Matt, Tom and Putnam. They let Putnam off right away, and the others are being held in detention. The other day Putnam came in with this big grin on his face.

"Just another two weeks, then I'm done! I mean, I'm coming back to inspect the job and finalize the paperwork, then it's back to civilization."

"Well, happy days are here again. But you know we'll miss you." When I said that his cheeks turned pink, like a six-year-old.

"The best news is that the sun's back! Almost four hours a day!" He cheered.

"I noticed," I laughed. "That's a lot of time for you to be putting in half-naked in front of the window. Hopefully they can't catch you from the highway – that much glare might cause a few accidents, eh?"

He laughs. "And where's Cheryl these days?"

"Oh, she's settling back into her place on Third Street."

"And the boys?"

Well, I grabbed our card and scribbled her number on the top corner. "Just give her a call."

Bill went ice fishing yesterday. Took the dogs with them, and when they came back Bill brought me a plastic bag. I expected his catch, which would have been very small, but it was this hat – black with a red stripe in the middle that was crusted over in something brown and nasty.

"And we found Davis," he said. And just from the look on his face, well ...

"Johnson seemed to think it was fine to just let the elements take his body 'cause probably nobody's gonna find him out there."

I opened the bag and took a look at the hat; it was the one I'd made, alright. "You know, Putnam said he'd lost his hat and his hunting knife before he left for his vacation. Someone had his things a long time before Davis was killed!" I said.

"How do you know he wasn't lying? It's funny, 'cause I have seen Tom a few times skulking around with another skinny kid, said his name was Matt."

I gasped so loud that Bill jumped. "Oh my God – it's the girl's brother! That's who did it!"

"Wow. Hmm... but we don't know that for sure, do we? Putnam could've easily led you to believe he lost his things because he knew he'd have to use the knife, at any rate ..."

"But nobody wanted Davis here – he was a nightmare for all of us! It doesn't matter who did it. I'm glad he's gone." That's when my heart started pounding. "Putnam? Seriously – it's all wrong ... he is such a decent guy!"

"You know this place does funny things to people," Bill reminded me. He came over and gave me a hug. When Bill holds me tight it's like he's a big bear and I'm his cub.

"It's all over now," he whispered into my hair. His big paws rubbed my back. Well, tears had sprung to my eyes and started making little wet stains on Bill's shirt. I didn't say anything, couldn't really speak, but I was thinking: I guess now Cheryl's gonna have a good reason to look into that legal secretary program.

That's when I felt Bill's chest shaking. I looked up and he was laughing.

"You think maybe it really was Matt or any of 'em kids? I guess you just never know."

The Boston Wedding

Theresa dozes in the back seat of Melanie's ghetto car while Paul navigates. Mel is the ex and Theresa is the girlfriend. Paul is the one who joins the two women like the strange Siamese connection that certain buildings in the city have. He has just come back from a conference related to his doctoral thesis. Mel had already arrived for her visit – picked him up at the Toronto airport and then they all spent the night before eating and drinking at a favourite pub, where Theresa and Mel were introduced and spent an inordinate amount of time bonding by teasing Paul. They shouted a drunken, loud, "Mutton chops!" together and giggled; the joke was taken from a picture of a Halloween celebration years ago where Paul dressed as Elvis during his peanut butter and bacon sandwich years – white sequined pantsuit and all. The photo was still on Mel's iPhone and she produced it for everyone's amusement after the second round. At the end of the highway is a wedding in Boston: tomorrow night there will be a reception at the Harvard Faculty Club, at least that's what Theresa's been told. None of them are in the wedding party, though Mel is one of the best friends – might be one of the people who'll give a small speech to guests by the end of the evening.

Mel turns down the grunge-inspired song for a moment so she can yell to Theresa: "How's the volume back there?"

Pearl Jam was good, but this band sucked. It's just too obvious when you're trying to sound like Eddie Vedder, thinks Theresa. "Could you turn it down just a bit?" She tries to keep her grumpiness to herself, squints at Mel in the rear-view.

Mel lowers the volume but she and Paul continue singing in a slightly constipated vocal style to the tunes from the disc player. Mel's jaunty ponytail bounces as she bobs her head in time to the new melody. Paul turns back to Theresa, reaches out and squeezes her leg affectionately. Apparently, I need attention, thinks Theresa. She's seen him all morning – peppy, jumpy: like an academic about to give the lecture that will get him a tenure-track position. Maybe what any man might look like negotiating between the friendly ex and the current girlfriend.

Mel slows at the next exit, changes lanes, and it's lunchtime. "Road trips are all about junk food," says Mel as they pull up to the multi-franchise restaurant building.

Theresa walks twice around the complex, comparing the meals. She goes for a cheeseburger she hasn't had since high school, finds Paul and Mel sitting chummily in one of the booths. They talk about their time in the master's program together. Mel accents the punchlines of her jokes by stepping on Paul's toeless Birkenstocks. "Ouch!" he says each time on cue.

"You two playing footsies again?" Theresa asks before sinking her teeth into the burger.

They laugh guiltily, stop right away. Paul has talked about the fact that Mel didn't seem compatible, was always a little too macho, or something. "She's the kind of girl who likes burly guys who know how to handle firearms – maybe because she's a perfect shot with either rifle or pistol. As much as my Elvis impersonation worked for her, I'm still just a skinny guy with a big brain and no interest in guns."

Mel launches into some of the details of the wedding ceremony that will take place within the next few days. "I didn't know this but Rob and Steph met when they were kids. They apparently went to the same summer camp. And get this: they had an event called "naked day," where everyone had to take off their clothes and do activities in the nude all day – even the counsellors!"

Theresa rolls her eyes. Oh, the eccentricities of privilege. She's given Paul the same look during functions they've attended: faculty parties where everyone's had a little too much scotch or dark ale and the repartee is fun and open until someone gets pompous, or the rare occasion when one of his friends reminds Theresa that she's not part of academe. Yes, she's the *appendage* – the girl who worked in the bookstore and ordered Paul's books faithfully, punctually, researching scholarly titles and, of course, getting them at the best possible price for him. Paul does not come from the private school, annual European vacation, trust-fund background that many of his peers have benefited from. As they laugh, she sees that Mel is joining in. Mel is not like the other scholars: she prides herself on her modest background. Her father was a man born and raised in Appalachia who became a cop in the same city where he'd gone to college: Memphis.

"Hmmm," says Paul. "Naked camp counsellors? That's every boy's dream!"

They get back in the car. This is Theresa's first journey to the States since she was a kid on a school trip to New York City. Nice that it's Boston this time. And Harvard. Wow. When she'd mentioned the wedding invitation to her parents they'd laughed and told her about the old neighbourhood she should visit while she was in the city. Her mother had visited friends from high school a number of times when she was younger. Not the high school where she'd been enrolled, the school some of them had been sent to after the decision was made to desegregate the schools. Her mother recounted the horrors of stepping out of that school bus each day in the middle of an openly hostile white neighbourhood, but she also acknowledged it was that school that was the first step in sending her to university in Montreal, where she eventually met Theresa's father. Theresa had heard stories about those days in Boston: how that period had become symbolic of the failure of desegregation.

The car continues along the county highway and it looks like the southern Ontario roads, but somehow more lush; the forests are thick and dark green even beside the highway. Theresa leans back, closes her eyes, though the two in front are still singing. She has already done some research on the city, decided what she wants to see while in Boston. When she wakes, they're making a final pit stop. Bathroom and dinner ASAP, French fries and milkshakes in the car as the sun sinks over fields in the distance.

They enter the city, circle the many roundabouts to Mel's place – a large apartment she shares with an articling law student. They unload bags in the vestibule, head to the kitchen and find a tall man rifling through the refrigerator.

"This is William – Paul and Theresa." William pulls his head out of the fridge and says "Pleasure." Everyone nods at each other. William is a half-foot taller than Theresa, some mix of Asian and White, deep voice, killer smile.

"Did you miss me, pookums?" Mel says in a saccharine voice.

William looks at Mel with a thin smile, then plays along: "Of course! I couldn't do without you, sugarbum!" He walks into the living room and turns on the television set.

Mel winks at them and whispers, "I love bugging him."

They sit down with beers in front of the TV set. Theresa feels the cold fizz of the ale in her gut. She gets up for bed, ends up with another beer in her hand. Finally, she is sent to sleep with Paul in Mel's bed. Mel has offered to sleep on the couch for a few nights.

Theresa wakes to the shriek of a car alarm from the street. She grumpily turns over and notices that Paul's not there. She heads down to the bathroom and hears a conversation coming from the living room, peeks through the doorway and sees Paul, wearing boxers only, lounging in the armchair. Mel is lying on her stomach, the shape of her svelte figure outlined by the sheets. "Good morning. How did you sleep?" she exclaims in stage whisper, not wanting to wake the roommate sleeping in the next room over.

"Good." Theresa is curt. There is a kind of intimacy between the two that shouldn't be here – it's something in the tone of their voices, in the attitude of their bodies. It's a remnant of the closeness of two people who've been lovers. Theresa smiles. She can't say anything. She knows Paul will only accuse her of being jealous.

They decide together on a loose itinerary for the day, since Mel wants to show them some of the basic attractions, especially the Special Collections at the Museum.

"Why didn't you tell her we wanted some time to shop and explore the place on our own?" Theresa asks when Paul returns to the privacy of the bedroom with a towel around his waist, his hair dripping from the shower.

"Why didn't you say something?"

"She's *your* ex."

"So? She's made a friendly gesture to both of us. We're sleeping in her bed!"

"Okay. I just don't want her to be offended. I mean ... I haven't seen you since before the conference. Maybe you haven't noticed but you don't hold my hand in front of her."

"I don't hold anyone's hand in front of any of my *peers*."

"Ah, yes."

"You better get to the shower or we'll be late," he says, a waver of irritation in his voice.

They head to the Old Port and Mel shuttles them around like tourists. In the subway, Paul asks, "Could we see the Museum tomorrow morning? Theresa and I want to visit some of the other attractions around town."

"Sure, I'm flexible. What do you want to see?"

"Actually," Theresa starts, "We were thinking of checking out the Museum of African American History."

"Oh yeah," Mel says, as if she'd forgotten it existed. "Hmmm." She nods her head, acknowledging that Paul and Theresa want to be alone.

"Then we can catch up with you for dinner back at the house – I mean at the party tonight," Paul offers.

Mel gathers her things and puts on a smile for Paul. "You have my cell number in case you get lost which of course you won't, right? And remember the party is at the Faculty Club. You remember how to get there, right?"

Paul nods. Mel waves goodbye and Theresa automatically feels the knot in her gut unwind. What is it about this situation that feels so threatening to her? She takes a last gulp of water before they leave their seats at the restaurant, then she takes Paul's hand. He lifts her hand to his lips and kisses her fingers.

In the old schoolhouse, the floors are white, new and unscuffed. The place doesn't look like it could possibly have existed in the early 1800s. Theresa reads that it is a restored building and very little of the original layout or architecture exists anymore. There are no scenes or pictures that make the history real: no personal accounts, no chains, no switches. There is hardly any furniture, only a few diagrams of the walls, some photos taken from the time of the schoolhouse. In an attempt to preserve the dignity of anyone who might be affected by the reality of what it presented, the museum has been perfectly sanitized. It seems something like a gutted memorial. Theresa and Paul sit down in the small theatre while a video plays a photo montage of people walking the streets of Boston, of children in the real schoolhouse as it was, of teachers and principals. The images are accompanied by spirituals and work songs. The voices raised in pain and sorrow cut Theresa, and when she turns to Paul she sees that his eyes are also wet.

They sit on park benches outside the civic buildings of old Boston, all forming a small cluster. Theresa blows her nose and Paul puts his arm around her. "Silly white liberal," she gently mocks. She understands how the spartan effect of the museum, in the end, adds to the gravity it presents.

Later that evening they are at the faculty building where the wedding couple are having a pre-wedding celebration. Theresa meets the family, friends – people who come from the right families. She stays at Paul's side, who relies on Mel to introduce him to the many people he doesn't know. The evening is dizzying, full of rapid-fire wit, charming people, small talk and long tales. Theresa turns through the circles of conversations as if she's being led through a ballroom with different partners. She loses count of how many glasses of wine and canapés she's taken from the trays offered by the elegant servers.

When they go to bed, Theresa finds herself undressing by the light of the streetlamp coming through the window. "Come here," Paul's voice calls to her. She feels his hands on her waist, pulling her down. He pets her like a cherished cat, kisses her ear and they settle in for sleep.

In the morning, she opens her eyes to find him looking down at her. "Do you think that some day you might want to get married?"

"Waaagh!" She makes her waking up sounds and stretches out further on the bed. "Some day, I guess."

"I mean, to me?"

Theresa blinks at him. "Are you asking me now or trying to secure a place on my ring finger?" She tries to keep the offence out of her voice – but nobody's ever treated her like a coveted parking spot before. "We'll have to see." She kisses him deeply, wanting to distract him, wanting to discourage this future talk. Then she remembers they are in his ex-girlfriend's bed.

In the Harvard Museum later on, Mel stays with Paul and Theresa for the first half hour. "I've seen their permanent collection a million times. Gonna have a chat with the program director – I'm TAing one of her courses."

Paul and Theresa are bewildered by the size of the Egyptian collection with its many sarcophagi and details of frescoes. They move towards ancient art works of India. Paul looks at them, slows down to admire the pieces. Theresa finds the sculptures lifelike, not in representation, but in sheer sensuousness. She wants to put her hands out and touch this period of the world, this lost place in which gods and goddesses walked, loved, waged war.

"I'm going to check out ancient Europe," Paul says to her. "I'll join you later?"

"Give me a half-hour lead – this is what my thesis is about."

Theresa has heard all about the dissertation, smiles weakly. She'll give him plenty of time. She wanders about the yogic sculpture, then sits for a long time on the shiny bench surrounded by the silence of the room, sitting like a statue herself after adopting a comfortable posture. What is this period called? She makes a mental note to do some research into finding books about sculpture, about gods and goddesses. This is what she'd study if she ever went back to school – which she had planned to do years ago.

She unfolds her legs and shakes them out before standing. Her left thigh still tingles but she pulls her purse from the bench and stretches, then heads to the Ancient Greek pavilion. In the room that feels like a copy of the Parthenon, she finds Paul and Mel embracing. Paul leans down to kiss Mel in a way that surprises Theresa – with great tenderness.

Theresa leaves the room as quietly as possible. She decides to wander around Ancient Rome for a few minutes, then tries to strike the heels of her shoes as loudly as possible, which is difficult in her sneakers, when she turns back to them again. She hums to herself, louder and louder. She'll say something to them – tell them that she saw and what the hell is going on. Or should she wait until she can talk to Paul in private and figure things out from there? She has to say something because something's wrong, because she wants to go back to school, suddenly. So maybe not wrong but right.

She turns around and enters the Parthenon, coughing loudly while pacing toward Paul and Mel, who are chatting chummily again. "Oh, there you are!" she says when they turn toward her. "Do you need more time?"

"I think we're done." Paul turns to Mel.

Mel nods quickly to both Paul and Theresa. "I know this great spot for lunch just down the street. Then we can go to the harbour – where the Boston Tea Party happened!"

At the city pier, the three sit down on the cement benches facing the water. Mel talks about the Boston tea incident: the men who dressed as Mohawk Indians, boarded ships belonging to the East India Tea Company and threw the entire stock into the water in retaliation for England's exorbitant tea taxes in the colony. Theresa lists all the other small rebellions that eventually sparked the War of Independence.

Paul and Mel look at her, stunned. "Are you one of those history nerds?"

"You mean like you two? I like to think of myself as more of a closet American."

"Never heard of it ... imagine someone being embarrassed to be one of us!"

"Oh – looks like you just found her!" Paul winks at Theresa.

Theresa laughs, since she remembers all of the history she's read and the history she's heard about first-hand. What about the neighbourhood where the desegregation riots happened? She wonders if Mel even knew anything about that time. For Theresa it marks the beginning of her parents, since her mother would never have otherwise gone to Montreal to study, and would not have been working the coat check at the jazz bar in Little Burgundy where her father, the Indian-Jamaican schoolteacher with a passion for Oscar Peterson, found immediately what had been missing in his life. Two years later, Theresa was born.

Paul snorts loudly at some comment Mel makes, rousing Theresa from her reverie. Soon, they are talking about his missing chapters and the research he needs to finish his thesis. Theresa admires his intelligence and the animation of his body once he starts talking. She has heard it before and his words start to fade. She sees him looking at both her and Mel, and understands that he is still in love with Mel. The problem is that Mel doesn't need him, and that's where Theresa comes in. Paul loves Mel, but needs someone who needs him. But did Theresa need Paul too? She liked his company and yes, maybe she needed to have someone as smart as he was admire her. But need was a cheap substitute for love.

Theresa had read somewhere that love was friendship that had caught fire. She recognized now why those words had stuck in her throat. Things had never really ignited with Paul. Courtship and dating had been a happy arrangement; marriage would be a matter of ceremony, a signed contract.

Theresa squeezes Paul's hand. He smiles. She doesn't know what to do, and in a sense, it would be easiest to do nothing. After all, there they are, sitting with each other, pretending – all of them. Theresa notices a terrific pounding in her head.

"Hey, I'm feeling a little woozy-hungover." Theresa stands up, has to steady herself. "Can I cab it back to your place and have a nap?"

"Of course. And you'll need a key to get in," says Mel. She reaches into her purse.

"Are you sure you're okay on your own?" Paul stands and turns Theresa towards him, puts his arms around her. She presses her body against him, drinks in the familiar smell of his aftershave.

They all step into the street and hail a taxi for Theresa. She gets in and turns in the cab as it pulls away, waves goodbye. She sees Paul and Mel framed in the rear window, both smiling.

Theresa has already planned her outfit, hair and makeup meticulously. She has learned to think ahead because of how difficult it used to be to find makeup to match her skin colour. Gradually, the cosmetics aisle changed to include every shade of makeup from ivory to mocha skin tones. She hasn't had the benefit of coaches or professional makeovers – only a day at the spa once, years ago. The one thing she has always had is a sense of personal style, an aesthetic that ranges anywhere between ghetto fabulous and gothic.

Mel is going with her roommate, William, who fades in a dignified manner in his grey suit beside her red and black flamenco-inspired outfit, her jewelled hair bun. They take pictures of each couple with Paul's old instant camera. After they wait in the shade with the photos, Theresa notices that the picture of her and Paul that Mel took is overexposed: their bodies just shimmering outlines.

As they drive to the family's renovated farmhouse for the ceremony and reception, they survey the mansions of the neighbourhood – each property a half city block. There are swans paddling around in the man-made pond in the garden. The sun glinting off everything creates a golden haze, though the late summer breeze is clipped with frost. The ceremony is short and fresh, with the couple exchanging only a few words. The bride's dress reveals the tattoos on her left arm and back. The bridegroom wears a vintage suit – possibly his grandfather's.

After the ceremony there is the announcement of the open bar. Everyone takes advantage in the garden area of the house, milling about, chasing the waiters with hors d'oeuvres and glasses of champagne. They are rounded up by the bride's mother, who gently guides everyone to the back lawn where the tents have been erected. People file into the long rows of seats, taking care to notice who is eating with which group at each table. In the end it looks a little like the school cafeteria – with faculty jostling each other at one end of the room. Theresa sits across from Paul, beside Mel, who sits across from William.

A five-course meal with wine is served. There are speeches. A flamboyantly dressed professor in a sequined, navy top hat and cummerbund takes the microphone: "Well, considering the unlikelihood of such a union within the Department of Art History ..." He pauses for the laughter that bubbles up around the room, "I'd like to toast the couple on behalf of the Faculty."

The dance floor opens. The couple take the floor and there is thunderous applause. Soon other couples drift onto the stage in front of the band. Theresa is tired of the banter going around the table; dancing is the alternative. She nods at Paul. He joins her and without a word they walk on to the stage, dance song after song. Paul spins her and they take a break when the band winds down. Mel looks angry and is almost arguing with her roommate at the banquet table. They appear on the dance floor for a couple of songs – Theresa notices that William twirled Mel exaggeratedly, needing to express the degree to which he hated dancing. Paul and Mel started chatting through one of the dances, yelling over their partner's shoulders. William winked at Theresa and they shared a conspiratorial laugh.

Paul pours more wine into both his and Theresa's glasses, his eyes still on Mel. "You don't mind keeping William occupied, do you?" Paul stands and takes Mel's hand without waiting for an answer. They walk to the stage as the band starts up again.

Theresa sits beside William, finds his eyes trained on a girl twirling on stage in a pink satin gown slit up to her thigh. "Well, if you don't ask her next dance, I will," she says.

"You'll probably have a better chance," he smirks.

"Do you want to dance?"

"Nah. Come out for a cigarette with me?" he asks.

"I don't smoke."

"Neither do I." He pulls Theresa up from the table and they drink the rest of his scotch. They hide behind the house, lean in to each other, and make up fake wedding vows:

"I promise to ignore your drunken follies, to help pay your gambling debts as discreetly as possible, to discuss all of your shortcomings with girlfriends and co-workers!"

"And I, in turn, promise to neglect you after the second year, to push you aside for the dominatrix in accounts payable, though I will at least offer a back rub on our anniversary when I forget to pick up a present."

While they're still laughing, heading back to the merrymaking in the tent, Theresa realizes with a pang that she does want it. Not the betrayal and neglect – she doesn't want the same old game everyone played. Was it possible that marriage didn't have to slide into the inevitable? But what was she doing in her life that *wasn't* inevitable? Was she living up to any of the ideals or goals she once had for herself? Why was she, after all these years, still at the university bookstore?

When they return, they find Paul and Mel laughing with the bride and groom and others. The couple is saying goodbye – getting ready to leave for their honeymoon in Hawaii. Soon there is a short farewell speech, the bouquet thrown, which Theresa catches with one hand. Mel pulls out a few flowers then throws the bunch to another girl in the crowd. Everybody laughs. Rice is thrown across the lawn as the newlyweds climb into a car dragging old tin cans from the back bumper. In gothic script on the rear windows: 'Just Married'.

Mel's car careens through the darkness on the highway as they head into the centre of the city for an after-party. When Theresa gets out of the car, heels awobble, she surveys the neighbourhood, the square, squat buildings and painted row houses. They climb the stairs to a brick walk-up. It's Edwige's place, and many of the people there were not at the wedding. Two black men drink rum and slap dominoes down on the table. Paul and Mel immediately slip into a conversation with Edwige. The lawyer seems to want some rum, but won't go near the table where the men play their hands. Theresa breaks through the crowd and takes two plastic cups that sit there, pours some rum into each cup, asking if it's okay. One of the men nods, the other ignores her.

Theresa huddles in the corner with William. She swirls the rum in her cup and practices some salsa steps when he grabs her hand, follows her steps and they both laugh raucously. He leads her out to the windy balcony, starts kissing her furiously, backing her against the wall. "You're making me crazy ..." he murmurs. "Why are you dating that stiff?"

Someone changes the music and there's salsa blaring. Theresa hurries into the apartment again and hides in the bathroom, thoroughly confused. She washes her face, reapplies some makeup and tries to breathe slowly. She opens the door, is assaulted by the noise and bustle of the party as she heads into the corridor then the living room, which has been transformed into a ballroom with couples moving sinuously across the floor. She walks over to the small group where William has already joined Mel, Paul and the others. She shimmies to Paul's side and takes his hand and soon they are dancing like they have never done anything but. In a few minutes William is cutting in and then everything starts whirling. They are outside and running on the street. William is taunting Paul, "C'mon Elvis, let's see if you can run as fast as you can karate chop!"

"The race of the Alpha males!" shouts Theresa, clapping her hands, giggling at the clever, silly name of the race.

"Ok, I'll officiate," says Mel. "On your mark, get set … go Alphas!"

The two men bolt forward from some imaginary start line. William seems at least a metre ahead, then Paul pushes forward. Theresa sees the figures in a tipsy blur in the dark. She wonders how drunk they must be to be moving at breakneck speed in a parking lot where the streetlamps are out. They disappear in an alleyway.

A moment later, William stumbles into the lit area again and waves them over. "It's Paul! He's hurt!"

Mel says, "Mutton Chops is down!" She and Theresa run out to the alley and find Paul lying there on his belly.

"I'm afraid to get up."

Theresa crouches down with her cellphone illuminating the ground and his body. His arm is out in front and there's bone protruding from the skin where it looks as if his arm is hinged in the wrong place.

"Oh dear God … Paul, I think you've broken your arm in at least one place."

"I thought so. I went flying forwards and tried to stop the pavement from hitting my face."

They help him sit up. He gingerly holds his broken arm.

"I shouldn't have dared you to run – we're both hammered … I'm so fucking sorry!" William tries to help Paul to his feet.

"Well, if I wasn't hammered, it would hurt that much more … and it's already excruciating!"

When everyone's loaded into the car, William drives to the nearest hospital. Mel assists Paul in the back seat and does most of the talking when any of the nurses or administration ask questions. In a few minutes, Paul and Mel have disappeared through the flapping doors to the O.R.

"Why am I such an idiot?" William asks Theresa as they wait.

"You were both idiots ... it appealed to his vanity so he had to race. Oh yeah, plus being drunk didn't help."

"Why are we both such drunken idiots?" He bangs his head against the wall again and again.

"It was an accident." Theresa takes his hand and pulls William away from the wall.

"It could have been much worse," she says.

"Why are you so fucking cute?"

"Why are you so fucking drunk?"

"I asked you first ..."

Mel came out behind the ultra-bright white swinging doors and told them to go home, that she and Paul would take a cab back later after the bone had been reset and the cast applied.

"Can I get you or Paul anything right now?" Theresa asks.

"You're a doll. Two coffees, black and anything sweet – donuts!"

Theresa and William are already heading to the cafeteria. William picks up everything and pays for the coffees and four muffins.

When they get back to the apartment William pulls Theresa to his room and they get into his bed. They are fully clothed. He kisses her chastely and holds her close. "Mmm ... You smell nice," he murmurs as he breathes deeply, sleepily into her hair. She can feel the weight of his arms around her and she carefully unclasps the dress because the spine in the bodice makes it feel like she's sleeping inside a shark. She pulls it off completely. Soon they are both asleep.

The next morning Paul walks into the kitchen where everyone sits with coffee and completely ignores Theresa as she gets up and steps in for a hug.

"I'm only up for some of the Tylenol 3s the doctor gave me. Unless anyone has anything stronger like opium or morphine they'd like to share?"

"Don't I wish!" William smirks.

Paul looks directly at Theresa and shakes his head. "How could you have ended up in his bed?"

Theresa looks at him, "You're one to talk. Think I didn't see that kiss with Mel in the museum the other day?" Paul looks at Mel.

"Theresa, that really was nothing … really it was –"

"A sign of things to come …?" Theresa finishes Mel's sentence.

"So then, nothing happened, right?" Theresa looks at the amused William, sipping his coffee.

"Well if no one else is, at least I'll take some responsibility! Sheesh, is there anything wrong with kissing someone and liking it and liking her too?" William stands up, takes Theresa by the hand and leads her out of the kitchen.

Mel glances at Paul and watches as her roommate slips through the door with Theresa. "I never noticed it before, since either me or Theresa is usually wearing a ponytail or bun. We have exactly the same haircut. Isn't that funny?"

The Package

Uma knew something was up when she started to recognize zucchinis in the grocer's bin. There were slim, elegant lengths, bulbous-headed ones that tapered slightly, curved ones hanging curiously lopsided, ginormous fat things, and small, bright green cuties, all happily mingling together.

"Tony!" she gasped, picking one out of the topmost box. An old man squeezing tomatoes at the next bin snickered audibly.

On her bicycle, while careening through her quiet midtown neighborhood, she mused about penises and whether she would've recognized the zucchini if she had a partner. She'd been considering ideas for her best friend's bachelorette party, and suddenly discovered her gratitude for the imagination and zeal that her life as a single girl yielded. After her return to the city from that hippie enclave by the sea they call Vancouver, she'd found herself in a gentrified neighbourhood a stone's throw from her old stomping ground in Brooklyn. She was finally ready to climb off the Ferris wheel of relationships with men who were stoic and unwilling to emotionally engage – the kind she tended to attract as someone who was often willing to accommodate any fault to become psychologically intimate with a prospective partner. She had been on each thrilling ride of love's carnival, where distraction met fear of success, need for approval met fear of failure, sex without love met fear of commitment, love without sex met fear of being alone, drunken and/or witty banter met fear of sobriety. Being single meant that for the first time she was finding the time and energy for pursuits outside of the demands of the kitchen;

she was building a business – a catering agency – instead of working as top drone.

Once home, she made a list of items she would need for Marla's party, and jotted some ideas for the way cucumbers, carrots and zucchinis might be prepared in a titillating manner. She had volunteered her fledgling catering business, offering the party to her friend as a wedding gift. Marla could hardly turn it down, having been her roommate and most devoted food-tester at sOhO restO years ago, when Uma had put in long hours as a sous-chef in Manhattan. Marla was her roommate at the time – an interior designer who'd rearranged and resurfaced the living room three times before being satisfied. Uma had ensured that the kitchen was always in order and perfectly equipped – though often enough, neither roommate used it because of the sOhO platters she usually brought home.

Uma had earned a reputation in the world of foodies within two years. When the word hit that she'd quit sOhO, she'd received some flattering offers from competing restaurants, but turned them all down since she'd already made up her mind to head out to the west coast where the air was fresher, cleaner, the sea and islands nearby were more scenic than skyscrapers and the men were perhaps a bit more rustic and in touch with the natural environment. She wanted a mountain man, and, from what she'd heard from the Seattleites she knew, Vancouver – perhaps Whistler – might be the place to find them.

The Vancouver west side restaurant she'd slaved in as head chef had already earned itself a solid reputation as an eclectic kitchen that put a vegetarian spin on classic French cuisine. She put in crazy hours, even Mondays, experimenting with new dishes. She prepared exciting tasting menus and took up the slack whenever any of the sous-chefs had little emergencies and could not make it into the restaurant. This happened with more frequency in the summer months. Uma rarely left the restaurant before midnight and was there for the 11:00 opening and saw the sunny weather of June give way to the regular rainy days of September. After about six months, she realized that she had not had time to even spend a day in Stanley Park, North Vancouver, Kitsilano or any of the other fabled places she had heard about. It seemed she had very little time to even sight these mountain men she'd heard of. When summer came around again she started taking an actual weekend off each month and fired any sous-chefs that missed a day too many. Finally, there were a few hikes through Stanley Park, a sea kayaking adventure tour on Vancouver Island, and in winter, ski trips to Whistler. Still, the rustic types were as difficult to track down as Sasquatch. Perhaps she needed to hire a guide… The pace picked up at the restaurant until she was once again putting in sixty-hour weeks.

After those years spent creating substitutes for egg, cream and even butter in various textures, Uma needed some time away from the madness of the vegetarian kitchen, and was anxious to start her own catering outfit, tiny as it might be, making food exactly the way she wanted – with a new menu of dishes she'd experimented with over the course of a few tasting parties where only her most discriminating omnivorous friends had been invited.

She strode into the kitchen craving yam frites with a satay dip. Her mouth watered. It was past the time she usually had lunch. The phone rang. She turned up the volume and let the answering machine get it.

"Hi, it's Hanif." His voice surprised her and she ceased hacking away at a yam for a second to listen. It had been at least a month since she heard from him – typical when he was in the whirlwind of a new relationship. "Just calling cuz there's going to be a fun party for *Slut* media tonight. And of course, you're the first one I thought to call … so let's get dressed up. Oh yeah, I'm doing some sex toy shopping later this afternoon – so if you're in the market for anything, you'll just have to *come* …" he giggled. "Call me. Ciao, bella."

She'd joked with Hanif about buying a dildo at her tenth month of being single – just when it seemed unavoidable. She'd had the occasional date, only one of which had been worth the trouble of getting partly naked. It had been with a stocky, dark-haired hotel manager, with a sensitive palate, good food/ wine pairing skills, and a very convincing moustache.

Soon Uma was taken with the ginger, curry and peanut flavours going into the satay sauce she was making. She whisked the mixture and poked a finger into the dip to test its perfection while mentally putting together an appropriate outfit for something called a *Slut* party. When the phone rang again, she expected it might be Hanif asking for details as to what she would wear. He would be shocked to find that Uma was prepared with something special.

"Uma? How's my princess?" It was Chucho. They kept in touch through sporadic emails over the year and she found herself almost regretting picking up the phone.

"I'm good, and you?" she asked.

"Meh."

"I got this great idea for Marla's bachelorette party," she said suddenly. "I told you she finally decided to marry that wanker, Tod."

"Are you having strippers?" he asked with a salacious voice.

"No. I don't think Marla's into that – but we are having shirtless servers."

"That's Marla – going half way. Listen, I just wanted to check that you received the package I sent?" He seemed anxious for a reaction.

"Oh yeah, got it," Uma's eyes flew to the den, where she'd left and forgotten about the box. More than anything, it puzzled her. "I'm not sure why you'd send one to me, though, you *have* given one to Susan by now, I assume."

"Why would I do that? She's had the real deal for a whole year now, heh heh. I've given a few of them away – not too many though, they take more work than you might think. Plus I need a lot of them for my next installation."

"Yeah, does anyone at the college know about your enterprise?"

"Are you kidding? They won't find out until it's in the gallery, unless you say something, but I think my secret's safe ... right?"

"Do you even *have* secrets anymore?" Uma asked dubiously.

"Well, I guess I've given away the big one," he laughed. "Alright, let me know what you think of it when you have a chance to *play around* with it," he teased.

"See you later Chucho, I gotta make lunch," she said.

Uma felt strange talking to him again in such a familiar way about his newest plastics project – a latex reproduction of his own penis. They'd broken up for most of the usual reasons, but the real ending had been his leaving to teach in Georgia at a small Fine Arts college, just before she'd decided to head to the great big resort wanting to be a city on the west coast. It was strange having a mould of *Chuchito, or baby Jesus* as he liked to call it, just land in her lap. His newest installation would probably be the thing to create either fame or notoriety for Chucho. He was building a wall with a large platform of self-made dildos of various colours and even some variation in plastic. It was, as he described it, an experiment in texture.

Uma pulled the frites out of the oven. Wasn't it wrong to use a toy that was a mould of your ex? Could that really be considered moving on? Was there some kind of etiquette book on this? She doubted it.

Hanif stood naked in front of her, testing her reaction, which she didn't give – except for a few sidelong glances. Then, she was trying to ignore the obvious as his package hung there, right in front of her face while she sat on his bed sipping from her wine glass, advising him on a suitably inappropriate outfit for the evening. They'd cab it to the club, but it wasn't a good idea to slut up *too* much, she reminded him. She tried to tone down the lacy frills on Hanif's selection of pieces, since his taste ran toward garish in lingerie. "This is just who I am," he kept saying when she offered a suggestion. "Then why are you asking for my help?" she asked.

"Because I need to know if something makes me look fat," he goaded.

She rolled her eyes at him. "Oh my God you're such a girl!"

"Sure I am, honey." He shook his limp brown penis at her.

Since Marla and Tod got engaged, after a lengthy period of dating, an intense period of *antiquing*, then actually buying real estate together (signifying true commitment to Uma), they seemed to cocoon in their condo. Occasionally, they invited friends over for dinner parties. They rarely went out, and Marla had become another co-dependent casualty – too attached to future hubby to spend much time with anyone else.

Uma knew Marla would never dare go to a party in any way linked to the fetish scene, which a name like *Slut* suggested, and Uma had to accept the loss of yet another one of her best friends. This meant no more lingering discussions, long walks and afternoons of brunch and window shopping. Now she enjoyed that experience with other friends, including Hanif.

"All set," he said, displaying his leather corset and mini skirt. "You know, this drag thing is still kind of new to me. I used to be just a regular fag."

"You wouldn't know," said Uma, finishing her wine. She pushed a hand into her purse and pulled out a range of lipsticks for him, then stipulated that he could not, no matter what, wear the same shade she wore.

"Why not, it's so pretty," he pouted.

"Come here," she beckoned with a bright red tube. He kneeled in front of her so that she could trace his mouth with the lipstick, holding his face steady with her other hand. "By the way," she said, "You shouldn't be asking a drunk girl to do this for you." She pulled back from his face, examining the shade on his fleshy lips. Uma was slightly jealous of his full mouth that held the colour so well, unlike her lips from which lipstick seemed to slip off immediately. "There, now you're even more gorgeous."

Hanif stood up, smiled at his reflection and put on his blonde wig. "Hanna's ready when you are – lush." He picked up her empty wine glass.

When they arrived at the club, they checked their coats immediately in a black-lit closet where a topless nipple-pierced woman smiled and took their jackets. Uma noticed the crowded bar and saw that her former co-worker David was already there, standing stiffly with one hand in his pocket and bottle of beer to his lips. He smiled as they walked up to him, gave Uma a once-over and whistled.

"I don't think I've ever seen you in leather … Love the corset. Maybe we can find a riding crop for you somewhere in the crowd!"

"It's actually PVC. Got more of a sheen. This is Hanif, by the way."

"Nice to make your acquaintance," David held out his hand and told them about the burlesque show they'd just missed.

"Whaaat?" Hanif was disappointed.

"There'll be another one," David said reassuringly, but Hanif was already wandering away to a group of people he knew on the dance floor. "Don't worry." David hugged Uma. "You're much prettier than he is."

"Thanks?" she smiled at him. There was something about the suddenness of his statement that made her consider that perhaps David thought quite the opposite. He hadn't sucked cock in years, and every once in a while, when they'd prepared food together for various business or social affairs, she'd heard him express a kind of longing for a nice, clean man. She'd told him about the party because she hoped he might be able to find something – even something light and delicious, just an aperitif, appetizer, antipasto.

David seemed to be staring at the girls, perhaps because of the costumes – though he had expressed a recent interest in women, had in fact once fallen in love with one. "But she was different from the rest," he'd explained. "Careful," she said. "Now you sound straight."

Uma scanned the dance floor when the DJ dropped a tune from her early clubbing days; the song had been released half a lifetime ago and she noticed people danced with extra vigour, cheering in recognition of a classic song … she was unable to stop herself from feeling seventeen again. The music brought back those years of angst and frustration, but there was something else she recognized, the sense of wonder, curiosity and innocence of that era, and then, the tangible sense of the loss of that innocence.

She grabbed David's hand and pulled him to the dance floor where Hanif was already bopping away with a tall blond man or woman, she couldn't tell in the low light, even with the bright blue strobe. But he/she had long hair that framed a feminine face, and small breasts that flopped about like sardines under a red shirt, in spite of her gangly frame and stodgy walk. David started grooving, having lost some of his inhibitions with the beer that he'd finished so quickly.

Uma was surprised at this willingness, remembering all of the times she'd invited him out, and all of the whining he'd done about not being able to participate in a straight environment. *You're just not allowed to dress and dance like who you are in a hetero club, you're supposed to know how to move the way everyone else does.* When she'd suggested that maybe it was his own sensitivity or misconception of not being hetero enough and that he should just enjoy himself and well, just fuck the haters, she had to deal with his cold shoulder for a week in the kitchen, which had made going to work intolerable. Now David seemed to be enjoying the party, shimmying with him/ her and giggling. Soon Hanif was standing in the centre of the dance circle and went through some stripper choreography while everyone whooped and laughed.

When the tune was over, Uma headed to the bar. She'd realized, in the middle of the song, that she was surrounded by boys. Sure, they sort of counted as girls, but she'd suddenly grown weary. She watched them all laughing together as they danced. What she'd been thinking of were men, men that were different from the kind of men that she'd been used to, the straight ones, that is. Somehow, she hadn't been interested in very competent men ... they'd seemed, well ... boring. But now all that 'opposites attract' crap felt to Uma like an excuse to indulge in dramatic arguments and sexual intensity that made for an exhausting, slightly nauseating roller coaster ride after a month or so. She once thought that if she and a boyfriend compiled a list of films and recipes that meant something to each, and exchanged it (assuming the other might be interested enough to actually watch some of the movies and prepare some of the dishes), there might be a possibility for understanding within a relationship. As it was, people got into relationships without any appreciation for where the other was coming from – entire emotional, intellectual and sensory landscapes went ignored. Why?

Marla had once given her a copy of a film by some famous director who'd died midway through the making of it. Uma tried to be gentle with her criticisms, but found that it was, at best, annoyingly simplistic. Then she tried out Marla's favourite risotto recipe and found that some combination of the ingredients, each perfectly fresh and tasty on its own, somehow ended up creating a sauce with a hint of the sour tang of bile. This prompted Uma to refine her recipe/film swap idea. People interpreted things in extremely different ways: just because someone watched or ate or in general *ingested* something didn't mean anything. If they responded to it in the same way, however … that was key.

David climbed up to the bar where, just a few doors down he/she sat on a stool, sipping a wine spritzer. Uma noticed him/her following David's movement with a hungry gaze.

"I think you've won the heart of that pretty young thing," said Uma.

"Yeah, *thing* is right," he smirked, "it's sort of cute, but I think I need a little more definition. I like to know if you're a boy or a girl – I hardly care either way – but I like to know which." David surveyed the crowd.

"I dunno, I think I know what it feels like to be both and to like it … I'm sure you know that feeling too. Besides, how do you know that he/she's not transitioning?"

"Wow, she's got a great ass!" David ignored Uma entirely.

"Where?"

"Over there," he nodded discreetly to a group of young women sipping cocktails and chatting beside the dance floor. The one he was talking about wore a pair of tight velvet shorts over fishnet stockings with a matching velvet bra and had pulled her long black hair into a high ponytail. When she turned in profile to say something to one of the girls on her right, Uma noticed that the girl had beautiful earlobes; a series of tiny diamond studs lined the bottom part of her left lobe. Instinctively, the girl turned back, catching both David's and Uma's eyes. David turned away and Uma smiled at her while the girl smiled back, one of her brows cocked in amusement.

"Looks like all of your dreams might come true tonight," she nudged David as the girl excused herself from the friends, slinking her way towards the bar with the grace of a panther. But when she stood calmly in front of David and Uma, she ignored David, addressing only Uma: "Is this your first *Slut* party?"

"Isn't it everyone's first? – I thought this was the launch."

"Oh it is, but there've been a couple of fundraisers. I only know 'cause I'm one of their writers. I'm Tara," the girl held out her hand to Uma.

"I'm Uma – this is my friend David."

"Hi David," Tara gave his hand a quick and courteous squeeze.

"So, what's on the menu for tonight?" she asked Uma.

"Something delicious …" Uma tittered at the directness of the question. She glanced at David, who nodded approval.

"Well, that's not too tall an order." Tara leaned in and planted a big kiss on Uma's lips.

"Yummy enough?"

Uma could only smile.

Tara took Uma's hand and pulled her onto her feet toward the lounge area, where couples sat close, talking and necking.

The two girls laughed. Soon Tara was stroking Uma's hair, and kissed her, which Uma didn't mind. She enjoyed the softness of the girl's lips, lingering with newness. It didn't feel strange, but completely … good. Tara moved her hand to Uma's breast, tracing the hard nipple she found there, while Uma's hand moved to the girl's lap, stroking the velvet hip, and the skin underneath the net pattern of her stockings.

They kissed again, then Tara pulled back and something caught her eye. "Your friend." She pointed to the exit. David stood there putting on his jacket, smiling at Uma, diffidently trying to get her attention. He waved to her quickly and then disappeared through the doors.

The bar announced last call and Hanif, lipstick-smeared but smiling, sashayed up to the girls on the plush love seat.

"Well!" he exclaimed, surprised to find his self-confessed 100% straight hag making out with a woman. "Where's David?"

"He just left." Uma continued to caress Tara's palm.

"Yes, tonight was a little disappointing." Hanif turned toward him/her, who still swayed like a willow on the dance floor. "But at least one of us is getting laid tonight."

"Two of us," corrected Tara, giving Uma's thigh a squeeze.

"Four of us – do the math, people," said Uma.

"As long as it's not all together," Hanif said with great disdain.

Tara slipped her hand around Uma's waist and held her closely as they stood outside the building for a taxi. Uma hailed a cab as one slowed just up the block. Tara opened the door and the couple slid into the backseat. Uma saw the streets streaking by through the window of the cab, the lights blended together, streaming like the milky way. Tara came closer for a kiss, then her fingers slid into Uma's blouse. Uma silently thanked Chucho for the package that he'd sent.

1972 POSTER GIRL

The woman steps off the bus, waits for the rush of people to clear the intersection before opening her purse and taking out a slip of paper: her husband's little map with directions for her. It is safely tucked away inside the inner pouch of her handbag which is perfectly matched to the taupe of her taupe, beige and brown wedge-heeled shoes. She looks around for street signs. The humid June air clings to her skin like memory, she pushes her hair out of her eyes. She unfolds the piece of paper with directions, tries to orient herself to the alignment of the map and again reaches into her purse, this time unfolding a pair of sunglasses. She could be a poster girl for the year, but who could guess the amount of trouble she has gone through, setting her curly hair in large black rollers with bobby pins to control the waves. She wears the fashionable mini-dress her mother would disapprove of. Just like the girls in England wear. The old lady wouldn't say a thing if she could see her: just her usual scolding frown. Except now she is in Canada because that's where they decided to go after hearing that it was difficult in London – the people unfriendly with signs in shops that said *No coloureds allowed*, and in New York, the cost of living too high. Canada remained an uncharted glacial mystery. Back home, the only reason people returned from Toronto: too cold! People went about their daily lives in the midst of blizzards – unimaginable snow storms, like a frozen rainy season. Luckily, she'd arrived a few months ago, in the spring.

Now the heat of June makes her heady as she walks the immaculate streets, the straight slabs of concrete so neatly delineated in the sidewalks with their rows of trees that perfume the air with sweet, yet unfamiliar blossoms. Streets work on a grid: everything is orderly – she likes that. Not like back home, where unruly children, goats, roosters, and cows roam the roads, where a wild minibus might run you down, where there was neither law nor order. There are streetlights here that tell you when to walk and bus routes that drivers adhere to, not like the minibuses with their reggae and calypso music blasting from the open windows, conductor hanging off the side ... and the other thing, the most important thing: offices work efficiently. Paperwork passed through a system of officials and people could get through – even ones who did not have money for bribes. You could earn a decent wage, and save money to buy things – many sorts of things, from dishes to purses to houses. You could educate your children and you could make a living. You could make a life.

She is two streets to Dundas according to her husband's handwriting. Should she take the bus that he's suggested? It seems like a waste, since the building is so near. She stands on the sidewalk, waits tentatively for someone – someone with a friendly face; anyone who even looks at her, for example. A white woman walks straight ahead, even as she sings "Excuse me," her voice strained with politeness as the woman walks on without even blinking. In the city – the Georgetown she knew – it was never difficult to ask a question of a stranger, until a year ago.

The last time she'd gone to town, before the riots, she'd asked a fashionable black woman at the market where she could find the Booker Brothers store and the woman huffed at her, calling her stupidy. The black people in the city were not like her black neighbours in the village who were as friendly as family. In the city, everyone changed up. Even the younger Indian girls would look her up and down in a sassy manner. But then the riots started, and that same sassy Indian girl could suddenly be the one to save your life if you were walking through certain parts of Albuoystown. Then a whole set of Indian businesses in the city were set on fire and the looting started. Big Diddee's bicycle shop was ruined and she and her husband moved in at the old lady's place. Shams, Big Diddee's husband, had been beaten and burned while the looters coursed through the store like ants, lifting every last thing away with them.

In truth, she'd been happy to leave that overcrowded house and all of its residents: her sisters and brothers, her own children and Big Diddee and Shams, a big hulking man with a broken arm in a plaster and part of his back swelling over the skin that had been seared off. He took Daddy to the rum shop the whole day and night, both of them drunk and arguing when they got home, Shams beat his plastered arm on the table when he demanded his food from Big Diddee. If she was late with the food, he pushed her to the ground with his sheer bulk and laughed like a crazy man. He scared the children, he frightened the adults! He never apologized for making the baby cry.

A car pulls up on the street and the man from inside waves an arm from his window. "Do you need some help?" he calls out.

She asks how long it will take to walk to the intersection she's looking for.

"It's just around the corner. I'll give you a lift – get in," he says, opening the door on the passenger side of his silver coupe.

The woman ducks into the car, smoothing down her dress and new spring coat. The man is older than her – maybe forty – grey hairs on his lamb chop sideburns with a receding hairline. He smiles at her, reaches over and pats her knee with one hand while the other, thankfully, steers the car. She is very uncomfortable. When he stops at the next intersection she sees her opportunity and jumps out of the car, slams the door without a word.

It wasn't a share taxi, like the way route taxis in Georgetown pick up passengers, each knowing the approximate route of the cab. They cost a little more than the bus, but were usually much faster and more comfortable, depending on how many people were in already and, of course, who you were sitting beside. Last time she was with her mother and Big Diddee ... they were on the way to the prison and could only find a share taxi on the road. It stopped and they squeezed into seats beside a pregnant woman and her two children in the back seat. Luckily, it was a short drive. She couldn't feel the heat, or the tightness of space, was barely breathing anyway. They were holding her brother and some other men from the opposition party. Big Diddee heard from one of the women at the Chinese restaurant that they were holding the men captive in the country jail. The military police had roughly rounded them up from the party office and forced them at gunpoint into a wagon that took them out of Georgetown and into the small village jailhouse.

She'd known something wasn't right by the way he looked at her as she closed the car door – like a fisherman satisfied with his catch for the day. Her heart was still racing. She was shocked at how quickly she'd reacted when she felt his hands on her. Did they have share taxis here? Her husband had never mentioned them when he explained the TTC and downtown. She won't tell her husband. She walks to the next street and checks the map, only one more block.

She fidgets with her short-sleeved jacket, smoothes down her hair already going to frizz in the humidity. A thin film of perspiration slicks her palms to her leather handbag as she walks up the street. What she requires is composure: the kind that stands up to anything. She takes out a kerchief and passes it over both palms. She hears a baby crying from high up in one of the apartment buildings. When she first arrived, the sound of a newborn crying made her breasts milk spontaneously – as suddenly as the tears welled in her eyes. She did not have a chance to wean her youngest. The news had come suddenly from Canadian immigration. They had applied when she'd been pregnant with the girl – her boys only three and four. Word came back that they were not successful, to try again once the baby was born, and they did. They were finally given a visa when the girl was five months old. Her husband went first, took the big airplane to see what was there in Canada – whether it would be worth moving their lives, their children, their dreams that were as plentiful and useless as overripe mangos fallen from the trees in high season.

There is no telephone in the village houses – not in the village at all, except for the bank in the next town over and some of the bigger shops. She received a letter from her mother about what was happening in the country, a month after she'd left: the rioting had ended – the British had restored order, imposed martial law. A curfew had been set. Her sisters couldn't go into town for work or school for a month because it was too dangerous – they could be robbed or much worse. Her oldest son asks about her, her mother writes. The baby finally stopped crying after two weeks, stopped trying to starve herself, still refused the bottle and accepted milk and formula, but only from a spoon. *Like she forget her mother,* wrote the grandmother. You tell me any child can forget her mother? She kissed her teeth, remembering the old lady's hurtful words.

On the morning she'd left the village, she'd woken early to get to the airport. She'd given the baby a last feeding since the girl was usually up, crying for her breakfast by five o'clock, prompting the roosters in the yard who crowed in sympathy for the hungry child. The boys had found out after the fact about where their mother had gone. She was glad to have taken an early flight. Seeing the long faces of her sons would have been too much to bear. She did not know when they would come to join their father and her, but as soon as they could afford a large enough place – not like the shared flat they were staying in now – the children would be on their way on that big airplane.

When the woman arrived in the city – dazzled by the stone houses and tall buildings, the speeding cars and buses, the huge, funny looking trees – she found that her husband had been fired from his job. He had almost finished his university degree from the correspondence courses through the institute in England when the application process was done, but once the visa came through, he'd had to leave the job he'd earned through years of schooling. Then he was on an airplane, a month later he was sweeping floors in a factory on the cold side of the ocean. The fiberglass he worked with gave him rashes. When he asked for another task, they fired him.

She is vaguely aware of the lack of the sea. During her first week there, her husband took her to the lakefront area and they'd had a picnic in a park where you could see the water. She'd noticed the smell of the water – damp and mossy, not like the ocean wind she was used to. There was a depth to the ocean air, you could smell time as it lingered at the seashore: different deposits of stone, the wrecks of old and forgotten sea vessels, layers of decomposing carcasses, salt, blood. Not that she'd ever been on a boat, except for the ferry she'd taken as a child to visit her grandparents who lived on one of the islands in the Essequibo River. She remembered how surprised she was that the islands never showed up on maps that she found in atlases. As if they were her secret – especially Leguan, where her grandmother forever made sweet bake and crispy saltfish.

There is the cross-street she's looking for. She looks at her hand-drawn map for the exact number of the building. As she makes her way to the other side of the street, she is mildly aware that her breasts may start to milk if she hears the sound of a child somehow during the interview, but the padding in her bra will take care of that. It would be mostly embarrassing to explain. Would these people understand having to leave children behind? She doesn't know. She doesn't know what the place will look like – where she'll be expected to function as a secretary. She doesn't know how to make coffee, unless it's instant. She doesn't think about sponsoring members of their families to come and settle into the country, though already the old lady was telling her to bring over at least one of her sisters and her mother-in-law had nominated someone too. She doesn't think about her brother wilting in the jailhouse until he was almost dead of dehydration – or the amount they'd had to hand over to the guard to finally have him released. When the police break the law, who is there to turn to? She doesn't want to think about the debts the family now have.

She does not think about how they're going to ever move into a bigger apartment when her husband is not working. She does not consider her brother being passed over for promotion again. She doesn't think about her mother cradling, ignoring, dandling, coaxing the baby girl. She doesn't know the boys' grades in school. What she does know: whatever this job requires, she will do.

JAIME AND ALICE

Jaime could smell the apple fragrance of Alice's shampoo mixed in with nicotine as she drunkenly reached over him to get the bottle of *toronja* soda.

"This is a new drink for me." She handed him her cigarette, which he took obligingly. She methodically poured some of the tequila into her glass, then into his glass, set the bottle down on the courtyard floor and added the grapefruit soda. Alice swirled the mixture in the glass and gulped some back, then snatched back her cigarette and nodded towards his newly made drink. *Andale!* She laughed.

Each time she looked at him, she appeared a little happier; her blue eyes were the colour of clear skies and Jaime loved to look at them. He could feel the bare skin of her shoulder against his sometimes, and, maybe it was him, but he could swear that she'd moved from about a metre away to the position they were at right now, where, every once in a while, when she was practising a new Mexican phrase, she'd pat his knee with delight for just being there to witness her growing vocabulary. "I think I'm doing so well 'cause I'm half-Mexican! Even though my mom never spoke a word of it to me ... It's still in my blood, right?"

He didn't know where the other gringos had disappeared. They'd started off drinking Coronas in the cobblestone courtyard with Alice: he'd seen them all through the large windows of the living room he and Arturo had spent the afternoon painting for the landlord. It was a three-day job the *dueño* wanted completed in two. Tired, a little sweaty and ready for refreshment, he and Arturo had gone out for tacos and beer. When they came back to resume the job that night he noticed that all the gringos that were renting the *dueño's* house had returned for the evening. Just at the point when he and Arturo were cleaning up and putting things away, he saw the gringo couple sitting around in shorts and T-shirts, their hair down – even the blond man who usually wore a pony-tail. Arturo kept looking at Alice through the large window with the view of the courtyard. "*Híjole, esa gringa es muy guapa!*" He held his brush up, didn't realize he dripped paint onto the papered floor as he looked at her.

Jaime had noticed that Alice's blue eyes seemed to meet his every time he looked through the window. When they were leaving the house, with all the paints covered, everything tidied up and tucked into a corner of the living room, Alice called them both over and asked if they wanted a beer.

"Yes, please!" said Arturo in sudden English. Everyone laughed.

After an hour of drinking beer and tequila with grapefruit soda, speaking a cocktail of English and Spanish, Arturo had left. The gringo couple had decided to go to a café a few blocks away, so that only he, the lucky Jaime, and Alice, the fake *mestiza*, were left in the courtyard sitting on the edge of the clay water fountain. The sky had darkened gradually, as the level of the tequila in its bottle dropped steadily. He guessed it was getting close to midnight, though he didn't really care since the sexy *mestiza* was sitting so close to him and, every once in a while, brushed some part of her beautiful body against his. And she was laughing at all of his clever jokes, even at some of the stupid ones.

It was at the point when he said that he should leave that he felt her palm on his shoulder. Then the warmth of her face close to his, then her mouth on his like a wet fever.

The next morning, Alice rose naked in the bed, her body still as astonishing as it was when he'd enjoyed it the night previous. He felt the hammering of a hangover and buried his head under a pillow, still peeking out from underneath to watch her as she slipped on a t-shirt and went downstairs. He heard her in the bathroom and then in the kitchen. He heard her climbing up the stairs slowly, the way he would right now: tired, achy from a night of tequila and sex.

"*Le duele la cabeza,*" she pouted like a child when she came through the door.

"*Ven,*" he called, opening his arms as if an embrace could magically make her feel better. It did. They slept peacefully until noon and flirted in the kitchen, where she smoked her cigarettes like a film star, and cracked open a can of cola right away before looking in the fridge for something to eat while Jaime's stomach gurgled with hunger.

They heard Gordon and Lucy come through the gate. The couple slowed down as they entered the courtyard and noticed that Jaime was sitting in the kitchen while Alice stood at the stove as the coffee percolated.

"Hi," said the gringa with a friendly smile, her eyes flitting between Alice and Jaime.

"Good morning," said Alice.

"*Buenas,*" Jaime nodded to the gringo couple.

"So ..." said Gordon. He looked like he was trying hard not to smile.

"So what were *you two* up to last night?" Alice asked, making both Lucy and Gordon laugh sheepishly.

Jaime stayed for breakfast, enjoying the company of the gringos and the English words that flew around the room so quickly in their conversations. He found that when he stopped trying and just relaxed, he could understand entire phrases. It was as if he'd woken up one morning and found himself in an American film. The story was simple: Alice couldn't find what she wanted in America and had to return to Mexico, the country her mother had escaped, to find a simpler lifestyle and a good man. She couldn't make beans, but the breakfast tasted good anyway – the eggs and coffee and tortillas – even if only because he was starving by the time she served him.

The other gringos joked about the buses in the city. "They don't even stop completely – you have to jump off!" They talked about transit in the States, where all the drivers had to pass tests and go through strict training.

"Very safe and boring!" Alice said. Life in America is not very exciting, she explained to Jaime. Then she turned to the others:

"Oh my God, I'm so glad I decided to leave. You know my ex is in Vietnam teaching right now. I never believed him when he told me how much fun it was living outside of the States. I mean, of course the pay is shit, but whatever ..."

Jaime smiled. He could no longer feel his hangover and sat quietly, listening to all the English, the new words swimming through his brain and making him smarter, bringing him closer to Alice. When he stood to leave, after three cups, Alice stood with him and walked to the gate.

"*Enséñame ingles*?" he asked.

"*Sí*," she kissed him lightly. "See you on Monday? *Lunes*?"

"*Hasta* Mon-day." He waved goodbye.

The streets were full of people strolling, milling about in the plazas or the markets. The sun roared. Jaime walked down to the small market near Comercial Mexicana and bought fruit, tortillas and beans. There was a billboard looming over the department store entrance announcing the construction of a Wal-Mart. What was Wal-Mart? Alice would certainly know. He wasn't sure what he'd done to have gotten so lucky, but strode to the bus stop feeling as powerful as a matador.

After work on Monday, Alice and Jaime saw each other only after he and Arturo finished painting. They'd folded up the sheets covering the furniture, mixed the brushes in turpentine and put away the leftover paints. They would be paid at the end of the week, once the *dueño* had a chance to inspect everything and saw the fine job they'd done. Alice had checked in periodically to ask if they wanted some water, or tacos. But food and paint and all the chemicals don't mix well, and the house painters – accustomed to working for as long as possible without eating – refused her generous offers each time.

Finally, the painters sat down afterwards and had a beer with Alice. Arturo left with a wink for his *compañero* and Jaime felt light-headed, not because of the beer, but the company.

Alice had changed into a pale blue strapped top which matched her eyes, and also, he noticed but tried not to stare at her backside. Her shorts were so short that when she stood above him he could see the faint outlines of underwear. She was laughing a lot, which meant she'd already been drinking. She talked about the company she worked for – how they exploited their workers.

Jaime asked if this never happened in a country like America. She was silent, thought about it and laughed. *No, pero pagan más.* Of course, that's the story of America. They pay more. That's why his brother set out to cross the border two years ago, died trying. Why be the unlucky bastard who finds himself on this side of the border? He never talked about Enrique, was surprised to hear himself telling Alice everything about his dead brother. Maybe it was the long work day and the beer and the company of a nice *mestiza*.

She put her arm around him, then led him upstairs where she held him until they fell asleep, fully dressed. When he woke in the morning he looked at her, embarrassed – he couldn't remember ever feeling this naked in a woman's presence before, especially with his clothes still on.

He got paid on the weekend and took Alice out for a nice dinner at his second cousin's restaurant. He got everything half price, though Alice didn't know this. They ate like royalty, even had some wine. Alice flirted with his cousin Pablo who kept looking at Jaime with great puzzlement, as if it could only be through some miracle that Jaime found himself a *gringa Mexicana* girlfriend. Jaime stopped himself from bristling with pride. He'd seen what beautiful women can do to a man.

After the restaurant they'd strolled slowly through the plaza, and bought ice cream. Gordon and Lucy found Jaime and Alice in the cobblestone courtyard, dressed up and practising *Cumbia* steps to songs on Jaime's tape. Jaime slowed down his movements so the other couple could follow.

They all spent the night in the courtyard dancing, until Lucy's legs buckled from exhaustion and she tripped over one of the large potted ferns. She started laughing maniacally. Gordon picked her up, both still laughing as he tried to manoeuver her long body through the narrow hallway.

Jaime and Alice stayed up way into the night. They watched the sun as it rose on the horizon and finally, they fell asleep.

In the afternoon, the sun and languor of Saturday made Jaime feel like sharing more of his life with the gringos. When he accompanied them to restaurants and even in the markets, people looked at him. He was no longer just a house painter, and with Alice hanging onto his arm especially, he became someone of importance. Alice sipped from her can of cola and lit another cigarette, gossiped with Lucy in the kitchen as he and Gordon chatted about activities for the rest of Saturday, and it struck Jaime that Alice didn't know anything about his town.

"*Vamanos a Hercules, a mi pueblo,*" he said.

"He wants us to go to his village – I think it's nearby," Alice explained.

The gringos all looked at each other, then smiled at him and nodded.

He took them on the long bus ride that headed outside of city limits. They stopped at a hilly range, a cluster of rocky outcroppings and challenged themselves scaling some of the more difficult passages before opting for the less rugged trail through grassy knolls. The grass trail led to gentler slopes where they rested under the shade of some Organo cacti and enjoyed a water break. Jaime picked up a piece of a black stone arrowhead that had been shaped by some crude instrument: the edges were scalloped, chipped away in sharp edges. He explained that it was made of black obsidian and that it had been created, before the arrival of that *maldito* Cristóbal Colón. "*Del tiempo de las Aztecas.*" Jaime said.

The pony-tailed gringo examined it in his hand then put it in his pocket. "Maybe I can sell it to a museum!"

Later, Jaime took them to the local *comedor*, where he suggested they try the special: quesadillas with *calabeza* and its flowers cooked into them. The owner looked Jaime and the gringos over critically, which none of the gringos noticed, since the wife asked many questions for Alice and Jaime to translate. The food was so delicious, Gordon rubbed his belly in appreciation, while Lucy and Alice smiled with pleasure at the blushing wife who buried her hands in her apron pockets. They passed a cantina with swinging doors and Gordon stopped and pointed, laughed: "Hey, doesn't it feel like some guy in a cowboy hat's gonna come crashing through the door from some brawl?"

"We should go in for a drink!" Lucy squealed.

Jaime shook his head vigorously. "Women no inside!"

"Women aren't allowed," Alice said.

"In this day and age?" Lucy said in disbelief.

"Yes," Alice nodded.

Lucy stomped up to the cantina and slipped through the saloon doors while Jaime gave anxious looks to everyone in the group.

"I'm sure it's fine," Gordon said unconvincingly.

Lucy reappeared with a sniff of disgust. "*Thank God* women aren't allowed."

From the town's streets, Jaime watched rain clouds passing over the hills they'd climbed. On a full stomach, days in Hercules were perfect.

Alice took his hand and they walked back to the city bus stop. "Come and spend Sunday with me too," she said. "And I can teach you more English."

On Sunday night they sat in the candle-lit courtyard, while Jaime listened to the banter of the gringos and their endless comparisons of what was different about Mexico. Rain started to come down – large, heavy drops fell from the darkness. The candle flames were whipped thin and out. Only the patio lights strung along the wall lit up the courtyard.

106

Alice huddled next to Jaime, made him take a puff of her cigarette, and then they went into the house, where they crawled into the comfort of her bed and she taught him new words.

When they finished the lesson, the rain flooded the streets, covered the windows in a continuous glaze of water. "*Tengo hambre*," Alice said, slipping into her bra and pulling on a pair of jeans. Jaime stood at the window and looked out onto the courtyard, noticed the small clay fountain in the centre – its water level rising rapidly.

Alice grabbed an umbrella and they left the house. A block away, Jaime noticed that both of their jeans were soaked below the knee. The streets were flooded. "It rains in the desert! Who knew?" Alice laughed.

Every once in a while they would see cars resembling boats caught in a swift current – the water up to the middle of the tires. They walked as fast as they could to the late-night *comedor*. All of the taco vendors had closed down for the night, and the streets were almost empty. They ran across the street and ordered *pozole*. A tall, handsome woman dressed in a blue gingham smock worked the small counter alone. She ladled the stew as quickly as possible. "*Esta lloviendo a cántaros!*" she said.

Jaime laughed. They slurped up the stew quickly and headed back to the main street.

Alice paused at the intersection to pull the hood of her jacket over her head. There was a man just crossing the street who ran without seeing the bus coming. In the next instant, they saw the man slip on the flooded road. The bus driver attempted to stop but trundled over the man as if he were a sack of corn meal. By the time the bus stopped and people were running towards the accident, Jaime noticed that some part of the man's body leaked blood onto the rainy street. The man groaned and gurgled at the same time. Alice made a nose with her throat and turned away, was sick on the sidewalk. Jaime ran to the man, watched his eyes close and noticed the way his arms and legs splayed out at strange angles.

They went back to the house after the body was removed from the street. Alice smoked cigarette after cigarette with the bedroom window open, searching the dark, wet night. "I can't believe he died right there – right in front of us ..."

Jaime sat on the bed and drank – not beer, not a mixed drink – tequila. He poured himself shot after shot.

"Christ, what am I doing here?" Alice suddenly mashed an unfinished cigarette into an ashtray. "I think maybe I should go visit Michoacan, my mother had some cousins there. Maybe we can go next weekend?"

Jaime hugged her and nodded eagerly. "*Sí, vamonos ...*"

They slept in the bed side by side. In the morning he left for work, tired and unable to concentrate. He told Arturo about the accident – also that he was going to ask Alice to marry him.

When Jaime went to the house the next evening, only Lucy and Gordon were in the courtyard.

"Where is Alice?" Jaime asked.

"She's gone." Lucy looked at Gordon gravely.

"When she comes back?"

Jaime saw the exchanged looks and knew immediately that something was wrong.

"She went to visit her friend in Vietnam."

Jaime went to the library and studied a map of the world, looking at Asia, examining how far away Vietnam was from Mexico. He wondered if he would ever go there, and how long it would take to get there by airplane. He wondered how much money you needed to go to Asia.

He called a travel agent and asked, hung up the phone with quiet shock. It would take many years of painting before he'd be able to afford a trip like that.

The next day, he returned to the house of teachers. He reported the price of a ticket to Vietnam to Lucy and Gordon, who sat in the newly painted kitchen finishing their dinner. They nodded their heads slowly. "*Muy muy lejos de aquí.*" They offered him a beer and he sat with them in the courtyard, practising his English – all of his sentences on the subject of Alice.

In the market corridors, strolling through the fruit stands and the *panadería*, Jaime no longer felt special. He roamed uncertainly, watched himself fade into the mundane of the market stalls. He sat at the bar, drank tequila.

A pair of gringas walked through the market wearing knapsacks, carrying maps. "Let's find the crafts!"

Jaime smiled at the pretty one with short hair. She ignored him. He was furious and slammed his drink onto the counter. "*Puta de mierde!*" He almost shouted. *No more gringas, especially fake Mexican ones,* he thought. When the nice weather came back around, he would take some time off, maybe go to Tampico, or farther south to Mérida. He'd heard that the Gulf of Mexico was nice. Maybe he would get one of those knapsacks too.

TRAVEL IS SO BROADENING

The jeep swung through another tight curve. Chris was still getting used to the manual drive, pulling down the gearshift if they had to dig in and climb a steep part of the main road that clung to the island's perimeter. The brilliance of the sun on the turquoise sea was disorienting. Transfixing. His stomach lurched with the panic of driving, or maybe it was the hunger. That was the thing about vacation – always going somewhere without sufficient fuel.

"I don't think we have enough food," Chris said.

"We never buy enough for you," said Nita, her arm leisurely resting on the rolled down window of the passenger seat.

"That's because I'm not a girl. I eat the same amount as you and Mom put together."

"So we'll go to the roti stand if you get hungry."

They stopped at one of the few intersections. Another rented jeep, a green one, idled just in front. Tourists in white, beige and sunglasses – the man with short dark hair pulled up in tufts of exasperation from dealing with the gear shift and wild bends in the road. Chris sympathized, noticed the woman sitting beside him in perfect composure: her sun-streaked hair smoothed back with a neat clip on one side, smiling at the view. "Pass my camera," Chris said.

"Now?" asked Nita, reaching into the glove compartment, unsheathing the thing and holding it so that Chris could take it when he had a chance.

He got a hold of it and frowned, passed it back to her. "Okay, you're going to have to take this one. Get the people in the jeep in front. It's so funny – the guy's a mess, but his girlfriend's sitting there like a fashion model."

Nita took a few shots, tried to make it look as if she was focusing on the landscape. She put the camera away.

"You know I'm kind of tired of rotis. They're great if you have them once a week, but every day?" Chris asked.

"Yeah, well, my forefathers ate that or rice with curry every day when they worked on the sugar estate."

"Those were different times." Chris booted up a sudden incline, switching to a lower gear automatically. The jeep stopped, then rushed forth with extra gusto. They were very close to the green jeep. The man in sunglasses gripped the steering wheel nervously at ten and two, and glanced at his rear-view mirror. Chris read panic in the man's face as he and Nita hurtled forward. They saw the jeep in front miss the turn and drive straight off the edge.

"Oh God!" Nita's mouth remained an open 'o'.

Chris stopped at the turn, then saw how dangerous it was to be stopping there. He pulled up close to the shoulder gingerly – as if it hurt to even touch the small patch of gravel that gave way to the mountain cliff.

Nita opened the door and ran to the spot where the jeep had disappeared into the horizon. She dropped to the gravel and crawled on her knees, peered down the hundred feet to the surf slamming the limestone of the island foundation. There were a series of ledges on the way down – narrow outcroppings of rock. There was no jeep or any sign of disturbance in the water. They stared down at the dark, tumbling waves. Nothing.

"What should we do?" Nita lifted herself up and looked frantically for any sign of traffic. A moment later a truck appeared. They waved it down. "There's been an accident!" Nita said.

The truck driver turned to Chris who seemed to have forgotten how to speak for a moment. "It happened right over here," Chris said, and gestured for the man to follow him.

In a minute the truck was off to the police station. A while later a police car appeared and two local constables stepped out of it.

Nita and Chris climbed back into their jeep by midday. They wound down the road toward Scarborough market and found themselves in the middle of a parade. At least, that's what Nita thought, until she heard a voice booming through a loudspeaker, "Who you gonna vote for?" A group of people shouted back.

Everything about the Trinidad and Tobago that she knew came from a five-year-old version of herself: the sun, the sea, picking out bones from fish in her stew, pepper sauce, ripe pieces of mango, goats on the market road in San Fernando, Buss up shots and ginger beer. She remembered the starched shirts of the uniform she had to wear to school – how quickly she'd dash home and tear off the clothes, put on her shorts and play with her friends on the street who had all done the same. But all of it was so distant – like something she'd read about in a book, or seen in a film. Like someone else's life.

"Who you gonna vote for, coolie?" One young man came very close to her, a hard smile on his lips. Nita felt Chris tugging her hand and they got back into the vehicle for an escape. Coolie. She hadn't heard that word in a long time, but it still felt like a blow. Even as he started the engine, the rallying cries and voices shouting political slogans echoed in the hot afternoon. Who cared about the election? Two people had died. But no one had heard about it yet. Life continued as always – there would be an election at some point after Carnival. People died every day. And it wasn't as though a couple of tourists had suffered some sensational and gory murder, more like they'd sailed off the edge of a cliff due to a kind of negligence.

Nita saw Chris's mother squinting up at them in her lawn chair as they pulled up to the house in Plymouth. Heather held her hand in front of her to block the sun as the brim of her straw hat tilted upward when they got closer to her. "That was a long trip to Scarborough market. They make you pick the fruit first?"

It was the fifth day of a two-week vacation and Chris was starting to feel the exhaustion that sets in when you're attempting the impossible: keeping both your fiancée and mother happy while traveling in the Caribbean. In fact, he wasn't sure why they were there. He'd wanted some time away from the office, especially since hearing some of the scuttlebutt that was going around about the CEO, who happened to be his father.

Chris wanted to spend more time with Nita just being a regular couple. Marriage meant change. Evolution? Devolution? Everybody talked about how things changed after the ceremony in ways they could never identify. But he'd also wanted his mother to get away from the daily grind that he knew kept her focused on what was no longer there; he wanted to show Heather that, in spite of not having Henry around, life was still good. And there he was telling her that in fact it wasn't good, just bloody precious. He'd seen the expression on her face go from amusement to horror as he'd described the accident. He entered the bedroom, found Nita half-dressed, lying on the bed. He leaned down to give her a quick peck on the cheek. "Jesus Christ, was that fucking close?"

"I know – could've been us!"

"I think I'm sort of in shock." Chris changed into his bathing shorts.

"Me too." She turned the other way.

"Come swimming with us?"

"I need a nap. Besides, she's *your* mom." Nita looked back at him before hiding her head beneath a pillow.

Chris snorted at the reminder, as if he needed one. He checked himself in the mirror: wide shoulders, a few sprouting chest hairs and just the beginning of a gut he dreaded. Swimming was just what the doctor ordered. He grabbed one of the towels from the closet and stepped through their separate entrance back into the sunshine where Heather stood in a pair of bermudas and her sunhat. Her brown bathing suit showed through the white fabric of her t-shirt. She led him through the laneway out onto the main street. "You know it still irks me that right now Henry's over there at his girlfriend's place living it up."

"He's been there for half a year now – and you're here, having a nice vacation," he said.

"I know you must be sick of all this, and I know there are people starving and children with hideous diseases living and dying all over the world and untimely deaths happening right on this island – but that doesn't make me feel better. What about my pain?"

"Look – you can deal with this when we get back. After all, you're in therapy ... Dad's in therapy ..."

"And? So are you." She glared at him.

"Yeah. And I could really use some right now," Chris said.

They came upon the blue horizon, and the sudden aquamarine stretched out under the cloudless sky made him smile. They were in Tobago. Sweet. He walked with his mother silently on the grass. When they hit the beach they both pulled off their sandals and walked to a flat area of sand that looked hospitable. Further down, there were people jogging and doing push-ups along the shore. The first time they'd seen beach workouts, he and Nita had laughed, then Chris found the section in the guidebook that explained how people got ready for the arduous physicality of Carnival. "Yeah, all that dancing and partying – it's hard work." Nita had said. Chris had taken dozens of shots of the people working out. Some of them had even posed – proving their strength by lifting logs and boulders.

Heather laid her blanket and towel on the sand, pulled off her shorts. "Well I'm gonna have a good time in spite of everything," she said in a pitiful voice.

"Atta girl!" Chris tried to sound enthusiastic.

Heather started wading into the water. "Think there are any sharks out there?"

"I doubt it – but I know there are a lot of fish in the sea." He laughed.

"Smarty pants." She shot him a look, walked in uncertainly.

Chris stood on the shore, kicking the sand, started skipping flat rocks. He watched his mother with a mix of admiration, guilt and resentment. It was disorienting for her to suddenly be without a marriage after twenty-seven years, but now he felt the weight of Henry's absence – as if he were now to step into the role, although he had a fiancée. Heather tip-toed into the waves up to her waist, splashed the seawater like a child and then dove deeply under the waves. Soon she was swimming, bobbing on the water, doing breaststroke and then front crawl. She climbed across the surface of the sea, leaning a little too much to her right, and Chris noticed that she was heading out pretty far, for someone who insisted she was afraid of the sea.

Nita woke to the sound of heckling laughter. She could see a few neighbours sitting on their front stoops through the partially opened slats of the jalousie window; they were chatting and arguing about politicians. She stood up and stretched, then headed to the kitchen. She inspected the contents of the fridge, trying to figure out what they could make for lunch. She'd been raised on the traditional dishes, and wanted to show them how *buljol* and coconut bake were made, though they could always go to the local restaurant or roti stand for authentic cuisine. She wanted to show them that there was an art to even simple meals; there didn't need to be big dining experiences in a country where everything was fresh, grown and ripened under the sun – often from your or your neighbour's backyard.

Nita pulled opened the bottom half-door and pottered about in the backyard. There were a couple of very tall palm trees leaning slightly into each other. At their base she found a few dried coconuts, and remembered a taste she'd almost forgotten. She looked up and through the lattice fence she spotted two figures – white people – dressed in shorts and sandals. Heather had a big smile on her face and nodded at everyone as she strolled down the street. Nita picked up the husked fruit and brought it into the house.

"Helloo!" Heather called through the front door.

"Shh. She's probably asleep," whispered Chris.

"In the kitchen," Nita said.

Heather and Chris wandered into the kitchen, gawked at Nita sitting on the floor with an old coconut grater, sawing away at the hard white flesh while the shreds flew into a large mixing bowl.

"Wow. Are you making a sacrifice to the gods?" Heather asked with a wink for Nita.

"Ha ha. I'm making one of the *trini* dishes – I think we have everything we need for it."

Heather shrugged, losing interest in the kitchen. She draped her wet beach towel on the bottom half of the door leading to the back porch. "I'm going back to my book …"

Chris opened the fridge door and pulled out a bottle of beer. He took a long gulp and burped and sighed in satisfaction. Nita stood up suddenly, squeezed past him. Chris turned around, searched for a sign of Heather, then pulled his fiancée to him. Nita laughed, struggled out of his arms and leapt to the sink, where she turned to him with a mischievous smile. "We got a date tonight?" she asked.

"Sure. Maybe we can go for a drive later on?" Chris wiggled his eyebrows at her, a come on that always made her smile. "Heather mentioned wanting to have dinner at the Crystal Vale Resort tonight."

When they walked into the resort, Nita expected they might address her, since she looked the part of the guide. But the hostess flashed a smile at Chris – recognized that he was with the two women in his life. She seated them next to a party of Italians whose bursts of laughter made everyone in the restaurant turn and admire their gaiety.

Heather smiled at them, and the man heading the table nodded to her, raised his glass before drinking. "I talked to the desk people about checking in maybe tomorrow afternoon. What do you both think of that?" she asked.

"Well, who would say no to this place?" Chris's brow lifted. He caught Nita's eyes.

"And there was a very nice Spanish man who asked if I like swimming, because they have their own private beach."

"Well … a very nice Spanish man," Nita hinted at the possibilities.

"Oh, he's probably married. Very few single people my age around here, I'm sure."

The waiter came around and they scanned the menu, ordered a sangria in the meantime. Nita had seated herself beside Heather and across from Chris. She arranged the flounces of her cotton peasant-dress, then reached under the table, pretending to fix her shoe, leaning over to give Chris a view of her breasts.

Heather gazed at the horizon, sighed deeply. "Well, this is more like it."

Chris agreed through a resonant, "Mmmhmmm," as he looked at Nita.

The waiter came around and placed the sangria in front of her – the frosty pitcher dressed in fruits and a small garnish of flowers. Chris poured a half glass for everyone at the table, then took out his camera.

Heather raised her glass, "Cheers. To a wonderful vacation." Click.

They clinked glasses and Nita noticed that Chris's feet were no longer in his sandals. He stroked his toes over Nita's as he took a picture of her twirling the flower garnish from her glass with a coquettish smile.

Heather sighed, looked around. They were stationed high up on the cliffs, with only the most exclusive rooms available on this level of the resort. "What is it they say? Travel is so broadening. Well, gosh darn, it's true!"

"Maybe we can get a tour of the place after dinner?" Chris asked Heather, straightening up on his seat.

"Yeah, their beach must be spectacular." Nita stirred the floating flower petals and orange slices in her glass with a spoon. "These are edible, right?"

"No. I doubt it," said Chris, examining the flowers in the pitcher.

"Sure they are. They're day lilies. Pretty – and peppery," said Heather.

Nita nibbled into one of the petals. "Hmm. Spicy."

"Lemme try that," said Chris, snatching the entire garland from the sangria pitcher.

Heather ordered another pitcher. Chris watched as she downed her first glass without savouring the drink at all. "Ma, I think you've had enough."

"I'll let you know when I've had enough."

Chris pulled the pitcher away from her, trading looks with Nita.

"At least you two have each other," Heather said morosely.

"Hey, let's ask about the tour!" Nita said, mustering up some cheer. "Maybe the waiter can help us out." Nita waved to him as he surveyed the guests.

"Oh, never mind. We should just go home." Heather erupted in tears. She stood up quickly and rushed to the bathroom.

"Everything's going well?" The waiter asked brightly.

Nita and Chris followed Heather and the manager while on the tour. The man wore a neatly trimmed moustache and, in a pleasant and efficient manner, showed the resort rooms, pointing out the décor and the many vistas along the path. He walked them through all three levels of the building and amenities. At the swim shop, he gestured towards the scuba lessons information written on a white board and asked if they'd like to see the private beach. Nita turned to Chris, then addressed the manager. "You mean the locals have no access to this beach?"

"That's right. But there are plenty of other beaches for the general public – for everyone," he said in a magnanimous tone.

The beach was a short stretch of pure white sand. Couples and small families lined up all along it. Nita saw Heather smiling at the tourists. She saw Chris smiling helplessly at the women: tourists and local. She wondered if she had a bias. It's true that for the most part she ignored the tourists, except if they were, for some reason, interested in her. She often saw that their eyes passed over her automatically, as if she were just part of the landscape.

Nita considered her family in Port of Spain and San Fernando. They hardly went to the beach anyway, though they might occasionally indulge in afternoon-long family picnics –

with food, beer, pepper sauce and, of course, a cricket bat. Nita wondered if she should visit her aunts and uncles. They didn't know that she was in the country. And would Heather and Chris want to see the other side of Trinidad? What interest would they have?

"All this stuff with Henry is fucked. I mean, Mom's right. He abandoned her a long time ago." Chris took Nita's hand.

"I know it's not easy dealing with all of this —" She stroked her thumb over his palm reassuringly.

"Your parents will never split. You don't know what this feels like."

Nita took Chris's hand and they strolled together along the beach that was reserved for resort patrons. When they got home, Heather stumbled to the house. "Well, I should get ready for check-in tomorrow. Goodnight, kids." Nita and Chris looked at each other, each wondering if someone should go after her.

"Where do you want to go for our date?" Nita asked quickly.

"Maybe we could just head down to the beach," Chris said. "Go get a blanket — then we can count stars." Nita sneaked into the house as quietly as possible, tried to ignore the sniffling sounds coming from Heather's room.

The next morning, while they were packing bags and checking around for forgotten items, someone knocked on the door. Nita was throwing away leftovers in the kitchen. She was the first one to the door and opened it, found two officers standing there. "Can we talk to Mr. Chris Garrett, or Miss Nita Ramsaran?" the tall one asked.

"I'm Nita Ramsaran."

"We just want to ask a few more questions about the jeep that you reported yesterday."

"Did you find it?"

"We may have found something."

"I forgot that we have pictures you might want to see …" she left to find Chris' camera.

The drive back to Crystal Vale was silent. Nita noticed Chris fumbling with the jeep radio as he tried to find something that would mask the conflicting emotions that hung in the air: Heather's loneliness versus Chris and Nita wanting freedom and privacy and the guilt that resulted from this desire. Nita knew Heather felt not like a chaperone, but a third wheel. She had seen her future mother-in-law go from being a broken, confused divorcee to someone who was rebuilding a life of independence brick by brick; she respected the woman's resilience.

When they pulled up at the front gate Heather jumped out of the car quickly and took her hand luggage from the trunk. "See you in a couple of days." She waved quickly.

Chris and Nita waved goodbye, pulled out of the landscaped gardens of the resort and drove down the serpentine road, heading for Castara. As they found their way back up on the high, winding road, Chris saw a few vehicles on the side of a ledge of rock near the water. They'd reached the area where the jeep had gone into the water. Chris slowed as a giant crane pulled up the body of a woman – dripping, hair hanging, clothing stuck to her body – dangling like a giant fish. They were about to lower her on the ground. Nita's stomach squeezed with the stickiness of dread, as if she'd relived some unpleasant climax of a nightmare. Chris started the jeep up again, ignored Nita's questioning eyes as he drove away from the scene as fast as he could.

Nita gasped at the view from Englishman's Bay. It was so beautiful that Chris parked on the generous shoulder surrounding the lookout – as if the road had been widened so that people could enjoy the vista. They got out of the jeep. Chris walked ahead quickly and stopped when he could just peer over the edge of the cliff. He sat down there, about a metre from the drop-off. Nita caught up with him. She stroked his shoulder as he wept silently, then lowered herself onto his lap. Her eyes filled as she gazed into his and they embraced tightly, tightly, in gratitude. The waves crashed against the limestone crags far below.

They continued to Castara in the jeep. The sun pressed down on them, made them sleepy, quiet. Nita kept one of her hands on Chris's leg, kept him calm, driving evenly. They didn't say a word until they hit the small strip of scuba-diving shops that lined the waterfront. Shop windows advertised glass-bottom boat tours, for those who wanted to see the reef area but didn't want to get wet. They stopped outside of a small rustic-looking restaurant featuring a dining room that looked straight out into the sea. They walked in, seated themselves since the place was empty. Nita pointed to a small island near the shore, with a lonely mansion standing on it. The waves were taking over the island, sweeping across the stonework walls, lashing the gazebo. A plump woman with bright black eyes, dressed in an old-fashioned gingham apron with matching head-scarf, came to the table. She held a tray with glasses of water and laminated menus.

"What's that house?" Nita asked, pointing to the island.

"You know James Bond? Well, the man who wrote all those books about him built that place."

"Does he still live there?"

The woman gave a long and loud laugh, "Nobody ent live in that house for many years. The whole island dropping into the sea." She laid down the menus. "The snapper is the special today. Anything to drink?"

"Carib," Chris said.

"You like the local products, I see." The woman looked at Nita and winked.

They all laughed. Nita ordered a Heineken. The woman nodded, walked away. Nita seated herself beside Chris, where they could both look through the frame of the window to the sea. "Christ, you think he made that kind of cash writing books?" she asked.

"Naw, probably while he worked for his majesty's secret service."

"Must be nice." Nita looked dreamily out the window. A calypso tune blared from one of the speakers hooked up to the corners of the dining room. "I love this song! It's one of the new ones for Carnival this year." Nita started dancing in her chair.

The waitress arrived suddenly with a tray of bottled beer and glasses. "You two on your honeymoon?" she asked, placing everything on the table and taking out her notepad.

"No, no. Vacation," Chris said quickly.

"The honeymoon's next year – after the wedding," added Nita.

"Careful you don't have too much cake before the ceremony," said the waitress.

Nita smiled politely, unsure how to read the comment. Was the woman chastising, joking freshly or simply offering some advice?

Chris poured his beer out in the glass and downed most of it in one go. His eyes swept over the abandoned mansion. "Man, everywhere I go, everything I do, someone like Ian Fleming's already done it. Can't even come to Tobago …"

Nita poured out her own beer meticulously, so there was very little froth at the top of the glass. "It's not about being original. It's about being happy."

They drove into Castara by late afternoon, just as the sun started falling into the sea. A middle-aged couple smiled and greeted them when Chris parked the jeep in the lot. Nita climbed out, stretched and yawned noisily. The woman wore her red hair in cornrows; her bathing suit was covered by a large towel wrapped around her thick waist, and she carried a dog-eared paperback in one hand. The man spoke German to the woman and they disappeared into the guest house. Chris could see down the hill to the beach: a few men were pulling a fishing net out of the water with so much effort it looked as if they were in the middle of a tug of war with the sea.

Chris took a small piece of luggage from the jeep and handed it to Nita. He heaved a large knapsack onto his back and they stepped into the guest house and checked in. Once in their room, Nita turned on the fan right away and opened the doors to the balcony. Chris collapsed on the bed, heard Nita sigh. He turned on the bed, saw the sun coming right through her dress and regretted closing his eyes, exhausted from the heat rising off the asphalt, the driving, the sun.

"You can see into all the little shanty huts on the hillside," Nita crooned from very far away.

Chris felt the heaviness of sleep weighing down his arms and legs. When he woke, it was dark and quiet, though he could hear the waves of the sea washing the beach. Nita's arm was wrapped around him. He gradually remembered that he was in Castara without Heather. A flash of a woman's body hanging upside down jolted him awake. He turned and saw Nita open her eyes. "You okay?" she asked.

He couldn't tell what his face betrayed – just knew that somewhere between the resort and Castara, everything had changed.

The morning light shone through the sheer burgundy drapery, casting the room in a cool glow. Chris shifted in the bed, got up to look out the window. Glorious. There were a few men gathered on the shore casting a large net. Waking in Tobago. Nice. He opened the balcony door. It was very early. He could hear a child crying, a rooster crowing (must've woken a bit later than the rest). He was ravenous.

"What time is it?" He heard Nita's sleepy voice.

They dressed and hurried down to the patio of the dining room. He scanned the menu. "Eggs and toast. That sounds good."

"What are you talking about? They have bake and saltfish." Nita said.

The waiter with his hair in short dreads looked them up and down, held a fist out and tapped Chris's fist with the bottom of his own. He brought them the island breakfast with side orders of scrambled eggs. "You two enjoying yourself here in Castara?" He smiled. Chris and Nita nodded yes enthusiastically.

"People in Tobago sure got a sweet life," said Chris.

The waiter grinned. He gave them tips about which beach establishments served the best surf 'n' turf. "You know there's a reef just out to the side?"

"Really? Is there a tour we can take?" asked Nita.

"Maybe, but you'll have to go back to town for that. You can take a little boat out, get you there in a few minutes. You can even swim there. We have snorkelling gear if you don't have."

The afternoon sun had just started its burn session when Chris and Nita waded back onto the shore. She giggled like a honeymooner, splashed him with one of the rented fins when they got to the beach. Chris noticed the fishermen were out hauling in a catch. Nita turned their heads when she reached the shore before him. She waved at them, and they nodded and waved. The fishermen turned to Chris and smiled. He gave his fins and mask to Nita and ran over to help them pull in the net.

The load was heavier than it looked and Chris felt his arms working, his torso turning and pulling. When the full net rested on the beach Chris saw the mess of fish flipping about, big sea fish, and a few small hammerhead sharks skiffling through the others at his legs made him jump away from the net. The men laughed.

"Dem sharks de good eating you know," one of them said, his gold tooth flashing at Chris.

They got to work cleaning some of the fish over a big basin full of entrails. The man with the gold tooth showed Chris how to hold and clean the slippery snapper. Chris thought about all those camping trips he never took with his father. His knife skimmed over the smooth fish too quickly, gouged him in the palm.

"Slow man, cool," said the man with the gold tooth.

Chris set the fish down and rinsed his hand in the stinging seawater.

Nita changed out of her wet bathing suit, rinsing it in the shower with her, hung the bra and bikini bottom on the stall frame. She put on cotton pants and a long-sleeved shirt to protect her from the sun's rays, and opened the balcony door.

Somebody was playing calypso music in the shanty huts. She pulled a magazine from her hand luggage and took a seat on the small balcony. In the distance, she could see the broad shimmering surface of the water, a wavering gold ribbon, connect to the sky. Just below, she had a perfect view of the road. There were two Indian women walking toward the shore, carrying their handbags on their wrists, their bangles jingling in time with their steps. They looked up at her momentarily. Nita could feel the women's scrutiny in the silent moment that passed, then they continued their conversation. Nita ignored them, pretending to read the magazine, her gaze only turned towards them again after they'd passed. They were headed towards the beach. Nita spotted Chris sauntering up the road, nodding to the other tourists sunning on deck chairs, swirling the ice in their cocktails.

"Hey there, fisherman," she called.

Chris looked up, beamed. His face and shoulders were red. A minute later he was stepping on to the balcony and Nita ran a hand on his naked chest where a few fish scales glittered, stuck flat to his skin. "You should have seen the catch! There were huge things like this," he gestured with wide open arms. "And hammerhead sharks!"

Nita smiled at his excitement. He leaned over and gave her a sea-salty kiss, left sand on her cheek.

"Buddy at the Seafest Grill told me to come by the restaurant tonight – and to bring *my woman*." Chris put on an island accent. He wiggled his eyebrows at her, disappeared in the room. Nita heard the shower, then his voice singing, echoing around the small bathroom.

They were on the way to the Seafest Grill when Nita saw the two Indian women carrying plastic bags filled with market goods and fish. One of them caught Nita's gaze, held it. "Good evening," she said as they stepped closer.

"Good evening, aunty."

"You know them?" Chris asked incredulously after the ring of their bangles could no longer be heard.

"No."

"Then why did you call her aunty?"

"That's the custom. But if they *were* my aunties, I'd send them a care package – did you see those hideous *frocks*?"

Nita didn't have to turn to him to see the dumbstruck expression she imagined on his face. She felt the shame of her words – it made her walk faster, as if she could escape what she'd said. They stepped along the beach in silence. Eventually, she slowed down. When he looked at her, she turned her wet eyes from him. "This is weird, being here. I guess for regular tourists all this poverty is just scenic and quaint."

"These people don't seem poor to me. Look at all the great stuff they have that we don't." Chris took her hand.

"You think they have libraries?" She asked.

"Who cares about libraries? Thinking about things too much just makes you crazy. That's why we're so fucked up. All stuck in our little heads ..."

They strolled up the beach, heading to the establishments farther along the tree-lined area, where music blasted from speakers positioned on the rooftop of vendor stalls. The man with the golden tooth welcomed them, brought them two plates of grilled fish, shrimp, plantain, peas, rice and dumplings. Nita knew she was hungry, but had no appetite. The surf splashed and trickled in to the shore, though she could only hear it in between the blaring reggae songs. Chris's leg rested against hers as he started eating. They fought over the pepper sauce on the table.

"What you want to drink? We have Carib, Guinness, and ginger beer," the man with the gold tooth asked, coming out from behind the vendor stand.

"Is it homemade ginger beer?" asked Nita.

"What else?" The man feigned injury.

"Two of those," Nita said excitedly before Chris could say anything. She turned to him. "You'll like this – way better than ginger ale."

Beenie Man's voice came blaring from the speaker, "Who am I?" he asked.

Nita started rocking to the music, picking bones from her fish. She leaned back for a moment, watched the sun sink into the ocean, dissolving in waves of light. It had been her cousin Sherine, in Port of Spain, who'd sent her a mash-up of Carnival hits and reggae songs, including classic lover's rock, Horace Andy, and Beenie Man. Sherine had married a black man she'd met at the bank where she worked. They'd gotten married, but no one in the family in Canada ever discussed her new family and it was only when Nita saw pictures of their first child that it became obvious that he was mixed, or *dougla*, as they would call him. She wondered at how the children looked today, since mixed kids were usually just more beautiful than regular kids – their boy at five years old and their girl now two.

"I think I want to visit my cousins when we get back to Port of Spain," she announced. "You don't have to come if you don't want, but I need to go."

"Sure, I'll come. It'll be fun." Chris speared one of the tiger shrimp on his plate, chewed thoughtfully. "Do you think it'd be difficult to live here?" he asked.

"You don't know what you're talking about." She laughed. "Paradise comes at a price. All I know is I'm *glad* we left when I was a kid."

"Well, I'd be glad to move into one of these huts on the hillside and haul in fresh fish for my dinner. Beats the office any day."

"Well, doesn't beat the law firm – except in the winter!" She took a swig of ginger beer.

Chris took her hand, kissed her fingers and waggled his brow.

Nita kissed her teeth long and loud, which had an uncanny way of turning Chris on, even though he knew it meant she was pissed off, or at least, pretending to be.

He took in the view of everything around him: sea, sun, fishermen, tourists, vendor stalls, Nita in a sundress. Breathtaking. He raised his glass to the man behind the stand, preparing plates for other tourists. The man nodded at Chris, his gold tooth flashing like a beacon. Niceness. That's what they said here. Maybe he could enquire as to whether buddy would be interested in establishing a joint venture – maybe run boats to the reef out in Castara too. Chris decided he'd be up in the morning when the cock crowed. He'd be out on the beach, casting a net with the fishermen.

Beenie Man's question dug into Nita so hard she retreated from her plate. She imagined Chris with his digital camera taking photos of every relative as if he were cataloguing them, instead of simply enjoying time spent with them. Then again, he hadn't taken out his camera since dropping Heather off at the resort, not even one snapshot of the fishermen; nothing since the police had flipped through and copied the photographs of the dead couple. Maybe Chris was starting to move with island time. Maybe he was ready to see the other side of T and T up close. Nita looked at his aquiline profile, then past to the foamy beach. Maybe she was the one who was ready to see it all up close and be his guide to an almost buried part of her: an unpleasant layer of shame the place unlocked, and underneath it, joy. She picked up her chair and moved it beside his. They sat together like an old couple tired from a day's work, watching the sea roll in.

Acknowledgements

Many thanks to my parents and sister Alisha for their unrelenting support of so many of my adventures, and to Sam. Much gratitude to K.M. and the Creative Writing Department at UBC, the folks at VONA and to A.N., W.D., M.D., J.L., and C.K. for their encouragement and wisdom. Thanks also to Luciano, Anne, Allan, and Kristen at Quattro for their guidance through the entire process, and to the Toronto Arts Council and the Ontario Arts Council for helping to keep me out of the dumpsters while living and writing in Toronto.

Other Recent Quattro Fiction